MARTA THE DOLL

If he would only guess

MARTA THE DOLL

by

ELOISE LOWNSBERY

Illustrated by

MARYA WERTEN

DAVID McKAY COMPANY, INC.
NEW YORK

MARTA THE DOLL

COPYRIGHT • 1946
BY ELOISE LOWNSBERY

PUBLISHED SIMULTANEOUSLY IN THE DOMINION OF CANADA

FIRST EDITION OCTOBER, 1946
REPRINTED JUNE, 1947
AUGUST, 1952
REISSUE FEBRUARY, 1958
MAY, 1959
FEBRUARY, 1963

Printed in the United States of America
VAN REES PRESS • NEW YORK

To

the dear smallest neighbors
LAUREN, BEE GEE, JOHN,
TOMMY *and* ANN;
with the Keyhoe twins,
CATHLEEN *and* CAROLINE

CONTENTS

CHAPTER		PAGE
1	Hanka's Heart-Wish	1
2	To Market, to Market	8
3	Happy Name Day to Hanka	17
4	A Cradle for Marta	27
5	Of Dragons and Cradle Songs	35
6	The Best Day of the Week	42
7	Dancing with a Doll	53
8	Which Is Best?	64
9	High Pastures	75
10	The Bandit of Bandits	85
11	Winter Fun	95
12	Star-Night	104

CONTENTS

ILLUSTRATIONS

If he would only guess . . . . . . FRONTISPIECE

PAGE

So they were off 11

"She is mine; this is my name day." 21

Marta was dressed for Sunday, too 45

Marysia danced with her two girl friends 55

Together they whirled round and around 67

They danced in high hats, stick-axes in hand . . . 89

Now Hanka could see the star 109

ix

CHAPTER 1

Hanka's Heart-Wish

HOW hard the rain fell! It rained and it rained. Hanka pressed her small nose against the window-pane. The rain made a thick gray curtain across the world. She could not see her dear Tatra mountains, though they were all about her. She could not see a single house, though on clear days the steep roofs peeped over the hills like big mushrooms.

"I wish I could have a —" There! She had almost said it out loud to the rain. Quickly, the little girl turned her head to see if the others had heard. But they paid no attention to her.

Burek, the big sheep dog, was asleep by the stove. He had not heard.

Grandmother was rocking the baby to sleep. She had not heard. She was singing, "Sh-h, now, by-lo, sleep, my dove."

But little Zosia did not want to go to sleep just then. She screwed up her face and cried aloud.

Mother looked up from her breadmaking. Her hands were kneading the good rye dough, moist and dark.

"Tst, my baby. Where is our little angel gone, then?"

Hanka watched unsmiling. It was true that usually baby Zosia looked like an angel with her sunny hair and her blue eyes and red cheeks. Usually she was so sweet that one could not help loving her. But today her face was red and stormy: she beat the air with her plump fists.

Big sister Marysia was scrubbing the floor. Now she wiped her hands on her apron. With the sharp kitchen knife, she cut off a little piece of crusty bread coated with caraway seeds. Reaching up to the cradle hanging from the brown rafter, she pushed it into the baby's mouth.

"There, little rain crow, don't fret your grandmother Babcia. The sad rain will not last forever. Soon will come the shining sun. Only sleep now, that's our lamb."

Zosia gurgled, sighed and began sucking the crust. The sobs ceased. Hanka turned back to her rain watching.

Now she heard Babcia's low song above the patter of the rain.

"Marysh always knows how to quiet the baby," Hanka told the rain. "Marysh knows everything."

It was true. Because Marysia was big and strong and kind, she helped everywhere. In the fields she knew how to help the father to rake and fork up the hay. Hanka herself could not help, but she loved to ride home on top of the high fragrant load. In the barnyard, Marysia knew how to milk the cows. Hanka could not help, but she liked to hold her small wooden mug for a drink of milk, foamy, warm, sweet.

In winter, Marysia helped her mother inside the house, cleaning, washing, cooking. Hanka could not help; she often got in the way because she liked to watch. How else could she learn?

Mother always said, "Marysia is my right hand."

"How I wish I had a —" There! Hanka almost said it again to the rain. She shut tight her red lips. "Or if only I could go to school with Jasiek."

For Jasiek was a big boy, much taller than Hanka, less tall than Marysia, just in between. In the Tatra mountains, it was not easy to go to school, so far was the way up hill and down. Today, with the road deep in black mud, her brother would be long in coming home. He liked his school, studying Polish books with the nice young teacher from the university.

He liked to tell Hanka stories, and she liked to hear —
about the people inside the books.   About kings and queens
of Poland : Boleslaw the Brave ; Kazimir who founded the
University of Krakow, who was so good to farmers that they
called him King of the Peasants ; Jadwiga, a queen at thir-
teen ; and Stephen Batory, first builder of big ships to cross
the ocean to other lands.   Oh, she knew them all.

She liked, too, to hear of children of these other lands ; of
faraway America where the cousins lived, or of France, or of
lands across the seven seas.

Hanka could not think what that might be, a sea.

"Made out of water," Jasiek had said, "just like our
brook."   Perhaps a sea was a great rain lying flat, instead of
falling down from the gray sky.

"When I grow to be a man," Jasiek had told her, "I mean
to ride on ships to visit those other lands.   I shall see how
they build their houses, their tables and beds.   I shall see
how they farm their lands, what seeds they plant, what har-
vest they make.   But always I will come back home.   Because no other land has such red mountains as our Polska,
our Poland."

It was true.   Hanka was sure of it herself.   She was certain, too, that no other little girl had so good a brother as she.
For Jasiek was never idle a moment.   After chores, when
the lamp was lit, he helped his father make furniture :
tables, benches, chests.   With his fine saw, Jasiek knew al-

ready how to cut out beautiful ornaments : flowers, hearts, leaves.

Hanka could not help. She could only stand close and watch how he carved a wooden goblet for milk, or a spoon holder to hang up there on the wall, or the milk pail to use in the barn, or the salt box to hang over the stove, or the Holy Mother and Babe on the shelf. Yes, Jasiek was an important person in the family. Father and Mother both said it.

Hanka liked best the days when all four children could go off to the woods to pick blackberries. Then she held fast to a big crescent roll. One hand grasped Marysia who carried little Zosia on her hip. Zosia pulled off her brother's round hat with its long eagle feather, and shouted for joy, while Jasiek let Burek his dog drink the last drops from the milk pail. All five were happy together. And perhaps Burek was gayest of all.

In summer, Hanka missed her brother sorely, though she knew that for him this was the best time of the year. With other boys and girls of the mountain villages, with Burek to help him, he drove the cows and the sheep high up and up into the mountain pastures. There they stayed the whole summer long, minding the flocks and the herds, making cheese. Sometimes the father or mother or Marysia went up for a visit. But Hanka must stay at home. She was too small, they said. As if she were a baby like Zosia !

But she was not too small to help. She could find Grandmother's knitting needle under the bed.   She could dry the dishes for Mother.   Or help feed the chickens with Marysia.   Or scatter crumbs for the birds.   On sunny days she could play house in her own castle under the big pine tree.   But today she could only stare out at the rain and wish from the deepest place of her heart.   She could not play with Zosia because the baby could not yet walk nor even talk.

If only Grandfather would come, that dear Dziadek, who lived with the aunt two mountains away.   For Grandfather was always full of music, full of surprises, full of stories. But he had best sit at home by the stove today.

"Oh, I wish and I wish I had a doll."   There !   She had said it out loud after all, louder than she knew.   For Marysia heard.

Now this kind big sister smoothed the little girl's brown hair.

"So you want a doll, Hanka ?   Like the cousins in far-away America ?   Like the children in Krakow or Warsaw ? I expect you are often lonely, with no one your age for play. Well, then, just you shut your eyes tight till I come again."

Hanka shut her eyes tight.   Did Marysia have a secret doll hidden away ?   Would she be like the letter said, with real hair, with big blue eyes that opened and shut ?   And a soft body to hug close ?   Oh, it was too much to hope for, surely.

Yes, surely, it was too much.   For just then Marysia told Hanka, "Open your eyes.   Hold out your arms."

Hanka looked.   She hugged to her the little bundle in her arms.   It was very hard.   Under the gay headkerchief, blue with pink roses, Marysia had wrapped a bottle.

"It's a doll for pretend."   She smiled down at Hanka.

"Oh."   Hanka caught her breath.   She smiled up bravely. "Well then, we'll pretend she has real hair and blue eyes that open and shut, and a soft body to hug.   Yes, we'll pretend."

So she closed her own brown eyes, so as not to see the bottle-face, and she began singing a lullaby cradle song, but softly, so as not to waken Zosia.

Now even as Hanka pressed the bottle-doll to her heart, the rain ceased.   The heavy clouds lifted.   Out came the sun to drink up the mists.   Up jumped Burek, the big white sheep dog, to thrust his moist nose into Hanka's neck. He even caught hold of the doll's dress with his teeth.   But Hanka lifted her baby safe, out of his reach.

"Down, Burek, down!" she commanded him.   "I know, you want me to go out with you to play."

But the mother said, "You would surely tumble into the black March mud and spoil your new doll."   She turned to the dog.   "Out of the house with you, there's a good for nothing, now.   Run off to meet Jasiek coming from school."

And Burek ran, splashing through the puddles, swish, swash, and shaking off the drops.   Hanka watched him go, telling her bottle-doll, because it had no eyes to see.

"Oh, if only, only —   Oh, how I wish you were a real doll," she whispered.

CHAPTER 2

To Market, to Market

ONE night at supper, Mother said, "Friday is market day, and we must go down."

When Hanka heard that, she opened wide her ears. For market day down in the big village of Zakopane was a great day for all the family. Mother and Father, Marysia and Jasiek spent the whole day before in gathering the things to sell. Mother made extra butter and cheese. Marysia gathered eggs, strawberries, mushrooms. Babcia picked a bag of feathers from the goose. Father finished a new chest, painted yellow with red hearts and blue forget-me-nots. Jasiek caught one of the new pink pigs. He had carved a new milk pail to sell. Hanka watched them all.

The next morning, she heard them discussing what they

must buy, which of all the things needed were most important. Jasiek needed new shoes. He grew too fast. Father's old sheepskin coat was worn thin. Marysia wanted a
new skirt for best, and colored wools to embroider Jasiek's
new trousers. The boy wanted a curved tool for his wood
carving. Mother needed a new butter jar; Burek had
broken the old one. Babcia would like some darning yarn.

"They do not think I need anything," Hanka said to her
bottle-doll. Though her old shoes pinched in the toe, she
did not like to tell it. In her mind she tried to see how that
market fair looked. For, though she had often begged,
they never took her there. Perhaps this time they would,
since her name day was so soon coming — Saint Anna's day,
the day after the day after tomorrow. So she asked if she
might go along with the horse.

"Oh, no, you are still too small," they all told her.
Mother said it, and Marysia and Jasiek and even Grandmother Babcia, too.

Hanka hung her head. "Too small, too small." When
at last would she be old enough not to hear it any more?

She stood on tiptoe trying to reach the big stove to see
whether she had not grown since last market day.

"Not quite tall enough," said Mother, smiling.

"We might lose you in that great crowd of shouting
people," said Marysia, "among all those booths."

"What are booths?" asked Hanka.

So they began to tell her with their hands, with their voices

— all at once — how along the road there are many small booths, shops, stalls with everything, yes, everything you could possibly think of to buy. If only you have the money, that is. Shoes for every foot, pretty skirts and jackets, big jars and small, books in Polish, baskets, kerchiefs gay with flowers and long with fringe.

"And candies, Hanka," her brother told her, "with gingerbread men, and cookies covered with caraway and poppy seeds. Oh, I'm telling you, it has everything, that market fair of Zakopane. Yes, even to a mountain of toys made of wood : dolls and carts and little men each riding a horse."

"And big dolls, too?" asked Hanka in a very small voice. "Soft dolls to hug?"

"Of course big dolls ; I suppose they are soft."

"With real hair ? With shutting and opening eyes like the ones in the letter from America ? Oh, why am I growing so slowly ?" Her voice broke. Tears came up into her throat.

"Don't fret," said Marysia. "Once I was only as tall as you. Then I could not go to market. But see, I drank my milk and ate the mother's good bread and soup. So I grew and grew and here I am. So shall it be with you."

So Hanka laid down her bottle-doll and began helping as much as she could. She ran to the old painted chest to bring out a shawl for her mother. She helped Marysia pack a basket with bread and cheese for their lunch. She found Jasiek's knife on his workbench while he put on his best suit.

So they were off

She ran out to help her father harness the horse to the big four-wheeled cart.

When Bulanek bent down his brown head, her father lifted her up to pat the white nose. On went the bridle, the round collar with its tinkling bell. Soon the shafts were pulled into place.

Now came two neighbor girls to ride into town. The cart with its bulging sides was packed full : people, eggs, butter, cheese, strawberries, mushrooms, a little pink pig in a sack, the gay new painted chest and the milk pail to sell, with straw for Bulanek to eat. Jasiek climbed to the driver's seat. As he gathered up the reins, Mother called :

"You have been such a good girl, Hanka ; we will try to bring you something nice. If there is a little money left over, that is."

She waved, and Marysia waved. The two neighbor girls waved. Hanka waved back, and Father and Babcia and little Zosia, too. Then, as Jasiek waved the whip, Bulanek tossed his brown head and started off down the hill. The wheels squeaked. The bell tinkled a gay tune. Burek dashed along beside the cart, barking for joy. So they were off.

Zosia began to cry. She wanted to go, too. But Hanka did not cry, though she blinked her brown eyes hard. She kept thinking of her name day coming the day after the day after tomorrow, and of how her mother had promised to bring something home from the fair.

What would it be? Once they had brought her some red candy, very sweet and sticky. But it had not lasted long. She had shared a bite with Jasiek and another with Zosia, and then it was gone. Once they had brought her a cooky with a lovely design on top. That did not last long, either. Once, even, they brought two carved bluebirds. Father put them over the door to bring good luck to the house. The wooden bluebirds had lasted even until now.

But what was Mother planning to bring today? If there should be any money left, that is. Hanka tried not to think what her heart kept hoping. But quite without thinking at all, without even wishing, all the while she saw before her eyes a big doll, with rosy cheeks, with blue eyes that opened and shut.

"No, no," she kept telling herself. "That doll lives in America. The cousins are its mother." It would surely be too dear in our market. What with shoes for Jasiek and the sheepskin coat for father, with the tool and the wools and a new skirt for Marysia.

The day seemed as long as a week. Hanka watched Babcia sweep the floor and make up the beds and fluff up the pillows and pile them on top. She scattered crumbs to the birds. But the finches and the pipits fluttered away. She began to make sand-houses, but they all toppled down. Again and again, she looked down the road. Her grandmother laughed.

"The watched pot never boils, child."

"But I'm not watching a pot, Babcia," she said.   She was only watching the road to see the familiar cart toiling up the hill.   They would all be walking beside it, so as not to burden dear Bulanek, the good little horse.

When at last Hanka heard the familiar tinkle of the bell, the familiar creaking of the four wooden wheels, she ran as fast as she could to hide in her favorite place, her castle under the great spruce tree.   Her heart was pounding fast. Her mind asked over and over again, "What will they bring me, I wonder?   What?"

She peeked out between the branches sweeping to the earth.   Now they were all driving into the yard.   Marysia was running to the house calling her name.   "Hanka, oh, Hanka."   Yet still, she did not move.   Were her feet turned into roots?   Had she lost her tongue?

Well, now came Marysia running toward the tree.   She knew quite well that it was Hanka's own hiding place, her own castle.   In Marysia's arms was a big bundle, wrapped in a shawl.   Hanka shut her eyes tight.   "What can it be?" she asked herself.   "Not a doll?   It couldn't be a doll!" Then she heard Marysia laugh.

"You'd best come out, Hanka.   Open your arms.   Here is a big surprise for you.   Shut your eyes tight."

Hanka came.   She shut her eyes.   She held out her arms. She opened her eyes.   Ever so little she peeped under the shawl.   Inside was a doll, a big doll with fair hair, as real as Zosia's, with blue eyes that opened and shut.

The child stood still, not daring to breathe. Suppose it were only a dream? Suppose the doll were made of cooky dough and would not last?

Marysia said, "I really don't need a new skirt now, after all. So I found you this doll, myself. It was made for you in Krakow, Hanka. Fancy that! Mother says we must lay it to sleep on your red bench until your name day. But I could not wait to show you."

Then suddenly Hanka hugged the bundle close. The doll was soft and real. And on the rosy red cheeks, she planted a big kiss.

CHAPTER 3

Happy Name Day to Hanka

THE moment that Hanka opened her eyes and looked over at her own small bench with the cutout heart, she knew that this was the most beautiful name day she had known.   Because of the doll asleep on the bench, the whole world was changed.   The sunshine was dazzling.   Jasiek rushed in to say that the stork had come back to build her nest on their roof.   Now the whole house, people and beasts, would be blessed for another year.   There was so much to do that for Hanka the day could not be half long enough.

At breakfast she beamed like a little round sun, her new doll in her arms.

"What will you call her?" asked Father, scratching behind his ear. "Surely, so wonderful a creature must have a name."

"Oh, of course she must have a name, and whatever shall it be?"

Everyone gave advice. Mother, Marysia, Jasiek, Babcia, all suggested a name. Should it be Kasia, Frania, Helenka, Stasia or Eva? Hanka shook her head. No name was quite good enough for so perfect a doll as this.

Father said, "How would Marta do? For the cousin in America? Then your dolls could each write a letter. You could teach her the *Ah-Bay-Tzay* — the A-B-C."

"Marta, Marta. Yes, that sounds just right," Hanka agreed. So, everyone was happy over the name. They called the doll Marta even without a christening at the big church. Marta was now the newest member of the family, even newer than the calf, newer than the pigs.

All the morning sped by while Hanka showed Marta her new home. She must see the big stove where Mother made the soup. The oven where she baked the good crusty bread. And the long workbench which belonged to Father and Jasiek.

"And these are the tools that make things," Hanka explained, "all asleep in their box. Only we must not touch the saws or the sharp knives, because men get cross when women touch their tools."

Marta opened her blue eyes wide. She seemed to nod her head. Now she was held up high to see the pretty cutouts around the walls. Marysia made them of paper with her scissors. Ever so clever she was, as Hanka explained. The strutting cock and the baby chicks were there, the wolf that lives in the Deep Forest, the deer and the big black bear. And lovely cobwebs to frame the holy pictures, and the Bandit painted on glass.

Hanka felt that her doll shivered a little at this. So at once, to comfort her, she showed to Marta the dear Queen of Heaven, Marya, the Mother of God. Jasiek had carved her of linden wood, and painted her robe blue. She held in her arms the small Jesus without any shirt on. They both stood on a little shelf made just for them, with a tiny canopy over their heads.

"And she is your Queen of Heaven, too," Hanka told her doll. "You may talk to her if you wake in the night with a bad dream, because never she sleeps at all. She has stars in her eyes, so never she sleeps."

Now when the whole house inside was seen, even the beds built in against the wall, Hanka must show Marta everything outside. Beyond the big wood pile for Jasiek to chop was the barn where lived the horse and the cows. After that came the sheep in their shed, the pigs, the chickens and the geese. They visited the bushes by the brook where the shy cuckoo bird builds her nest. And best and last of all the castle under the low-spreading spruce.

Now however the news of Marta's coming spread by afternoon, who can say ? Perhaps the larks or the swallows carried it. Perhaps the wind. But just as Hanka was carrying out her small red bench and Babcia's old shawl to play house, little girls began coming out of the steep-roofed houses nestling among the hills. Out of this house and that came little girls, running along the road to Hanka's house.

She saw them coming and ran to meet them. Burek saw them, too. He leaped ahead barking furiously, as if they were robbers.

The children stopped. "Will he bite ?" they called.

"Down, Burek, down !" Hanka commanded. "See, these are our friends. Sit now, do. No, he will not bite," she called.

So Burek must sit beside his small mistress, on guard, as the first little girls ran forward.

"Oh, what a beautiful doll !"

"Oh, Hanka, is it yours ?"

"Yes, she is mine, because this is my name day : but you may hold her."

Burek made a leap. He grabbed one cloth foot.

"Down, Burek ! How dare you bite her little foot ? Bad dog !"

Burek hung his head and drew his long tail between his legs. He put one paw over his ears, as if to rub out the

"*She is mine; this is my name day.*"

sound of that voice. He did not like to be scolded. But that new plaything in their arms, what fun to play with it. Just the sort of soft thing he liked to shake. And so easy to leap up on the shoulders of children and knock them down. It was not easy to be good. His brown eyes shone with mischief. His mouth smiled at the corner. Still, he had to obey.

Now the children disappeared into the castle to play. Burek was not allowed in, so he contented himself with running around and around the big tree, sniffing and begging to share in the fun. Whenever another child came running along the road, from uphill or down, he ran to meet her, barking a glad welcome, wagging his tail.

Soon the castle was full to overflowing. The children played house. Each took a turn minding the new baby. They put her to sleep. They took off her dress and laid her on the bench. They woke her up and put her dress on again. They wrapped her in the shawl as if it were winter. They looked at her white petticoats, very full and edged with lace. What a wonderful, beautiful doll! Lucky Hanka, to have a birthday so near her name day for Saint Anna, for the mother of the mother of Pan Jezus. Lucky Hanka, to be named for the very saint who is patroness of all mountain folk!

All the children thought they might like to stay forever at Hanka's house, just to play all the day long with such a doll.

But then came Marysia, bending low, parting the fragrant

green branches, greeting this one and that. In her right hand she carried a pail, in her left a basket covered over with a white cloth. When she opened it, a delicious fragrance floated out.

"Who would like a honey cake?" She smiled at them all, their faces flushed like roses in the dim green light. "Hanka's mother just baked them for you. And here is a mug for a drink of good sour milk."

"And we won't forget to give Marta some, too," said Hanka, helping to pass the full mug.

"Of course Marta must have some, too," Marysia agreed.

All the children agreed. Each broke off a corner of her honey cake for those smiling red lips.

But then in came Burek after all. Sniffing that fragrance, he could not help squirming through. And all the crumbs that Marta left Burek gobbled up, leaving only a few for the birds. For thanks, he licked Marta's pink cheeks until she blushed at his rough red tongue. He pulled her dress. What a sweet thing she was! So thought every little girl as each took turns holding her one last time.

For Marysia said the sun would soon be dropping down into the valleys below. He would visit Zakopane and then go to sleep under the sea. So then, it was time that the children be up on the road and off home else mothers would be anxious. Yes, Hanka and Marta might walk a little way along the road, and Marysia and Burek came, too. It was hard to part.

"Now then," said Marysia, "pretend you are leaves scurrying off before the north wind. But you may come another day to play with Hanka and her doll."

Burek barked his farewell. Hanka waved Marta's arm.

"Good-bye, Hanka. Good-bye, Marta, dear," the voices called. Then some ran up the hill and some ran down.

As the sisters turned back, Hanka gave Marysia her hand. She looked at her new doll wrapped safely in the ends of her own shawl.

"Oh, you are good to me, Marysia," she said. "And I will be good to Marta. I will take such care of her. And I will keep her as long as I live."

"And when you have a little girl who longs for a doll, you will go to your own painted chest. You will search down under the best dress for Sundays, to find a bundle wrapped in an old flowery shawl. You will put it into your little girl's arms and say, 'Here, my child, here is a doll made in Krakow that was your mother's first doll.'"

"Yes," Hanka agreed. "That is how it will be."

She was so happy that she could hardly eat her soup. The day had been so full. Her eyes just would droop shut. Mother helped her early to bed. But just as she was nearly asleep standing up, she thought, "Wherever will I put Marta to sleep? I have a corner of Marysia's bed, Zosia has her cradle. But Marta has only my hard red bench."

Hanka was so tired that she began to weep. It seemed all at once a real trouble. Who could mend it? Not Mother, not Babcia, nor even Marysia. But Jasiek lifted her gloom.

"As if one crybaby were not enough for our family ! As if a bench were not good enough for Marta, as it is every night for me ! Well then, if Miss Marta must have a private bed, why, I suppose I must give her my toolbox."

Mother smiled. "You cannot learn younger to care for a lady, my son."

"Yes," agreed Marysia, tousling her brother's fair hair. "Soon you 'll be taking a lady to care for all the rest of your life."

Jasiek flushed. He emptied out his tools with a clatter. He brought the box to Hanka. Yes, just the thing for a very small child, just her size. Now Marta could rest here, beside her own bed, covered with the old shawl. No, Burek would not take the doll, they assured her. He was not allowed. He would spend the night in the barn to guard the horse and the cows, to guard the geese, the hens, the sheep and the pigs ; to guard all the family and even Marta, too.

So all was well. Both Hanka and Marta shut their eyes fast. And they could hardly wait for tomorrow.

CHAPTER 4

A Cradle for Marta

NOW began a new life for Hanka. Little sister Zosia had three mothers, for Babcia and Marysia helped Mother to take care of the child. But Marta had only one little mother. And that one was Hanka.

What good care she took of her doll. As she brushed the fair hair, she talked to her. She told Marta all her dreams. She explained things; how the sun climbed up over the high snowy mountains and traveled across the blue sky by day, and the moon by night. Why the shining stars rested upon the dark Tatra peaks.

Whatever Hanka knew, that she told to Marta. And she

was pleased when the doll looked back at her very knowingly out of the big wide-open blue eyes. "Truly," Hanka thought, "she must be glad to hear all that I have in my heart to tell her, for how else can she learn about this beautiful land called Poland?"

Big sister Marysia said, "As our mother cares for you, so shall you care for Marta. She will not like being carried about upside down. She will not like being dropped in the hot ashes of the hearth."

"Of course I shall take good care of my new doll," said Hanka. "Am I not her mother?"

When Zosia took a nap, Marta took one, too. Hanka put her into the toolbox, and covered her with a shawl. Now she took her out again. For it came to her that a toolbox instead of a proper cradle was no better than a bottle instead of a real doll. She had no sooner thought this than she began looking up the road, wishing for Jasiek to come home from school. She ran out to hide in the castle until she heard his axe chopping wood.

Now, carrying Marta in the box, she went out to the yard. She stood as close to the boy as she could, looking up into his face. If only he would guess. If only he could read her thoughts. Then she need not have to ask him. For Hanka was shy, for all that her brother had a good straight gentle look in his blue eyes under the long lashes.

"Chop, chopity chop," sang the axe, swinging with the might of his young arms.

"Crack, crick crack," sang the wood. How white it was inside, and how fragrant the red pine chips.

Hanka filled one end of the box with them. "If we feed them to the fire, then they will put the fire-fairies' babies to sleep," she told her doll.

Still, Jasiek did not speak, but went on steadily chopping wood. So Hanka would have to. She cleared her throat.

"Jas, do you know that Marta is more than a doll, that she is often my baby?"

Jasiek snorted. "All girls like babies," he said shortly, between mighty strokes of his sharp axe. "Mind you stand back else I might chop off her head!"

Hanka quickly stepped back.

"Chop, chopity chop," sang the axe.

If only Jasiek would guess what she meant. She must try again.

"Well then, since Marta is my baby, my real baby, don't you think she needs a cradle to sleep in, please?" There! It was out.

"Poof! I suppose my best toolbox is not good enough for her. I suppose she needs a golden bed like a princess in a fairy tale."

So, now he was getting a little warm, even if he was teasing her. Hanka looked at his strong hands, at the wide swing of his axe, silver-bright with much polishing. Wistfully, she sighed.

"You made Mother a beautiful spoon holder," Hanka

reminded him. "And you helped Father to make the cradle for Zosia. Only hers does not rock."

"No, because Mother wanted it to hang down from above, that's why. But of course we could make it rock, if we liked."

Oh! Would he never guess? After a bit, Hanka edged nearer. She asked in a small voice without looking at him, "Jas, how would you like to have back your toolbox? And how would you like to make a real cradle for Marta, please? One that rocks? One just her size."

Jasiek put down his axe. He began to laugh in his hearty loud way. So now Hanka laughed, too. For she knew that if Jas laughed, he must mean well. He would surely make it then. She nodded to Marta. Marta did not laugh out loud, she just stared up at Jas, but her mouth looked so rosy and smiling that she seemed just on the point of thanking him, too.

When the wood was all piled up and taken into the kitchen-end, with Hanka helping all she could, Jasiek bent over his work bench. Hanka stood beside him in the window.

"Well then," said Jasiek, "can I see if you shut out all the light?" His voice sounded cross. So Hanka stood aside. She put Marta into her box for a nap, and covered her up. Perhaps she could help. If only Jas would begin the cradle now!

"Now then," said Jasiek, "for the sides, I think this

smooth board will do. Good willow, dry and light." His voice was not cross, now. He measured the toolbox. He measured his board. "Give me the saw — no, that one, over there."

Hanka brought the saw, even without please.

"Now, bring me the hammer."

She brought the hammer, without the please.

"Now bring me the nails — no, those smallest ones, there."

Hanka brought him the nails. Now she watched breathlessly as with a stub of black pencil, he drew on his white board a rounding curve. He stood back studying his work. He half shut his eyes. Hanka was astonished. He looked as if he were seeing the cradle behind his eyes, in the place where his mind must be. But how could he see with his mind?

"Probably, just as I saw Marta, before ever she came to live with me," she thought.

She saw him rub out his curve, draw another. He measured carefully with a ruler. A curving line between two straight ones, slanted just so. Whatever was that for? That couldn't be a cradle.

"That will do it," said Jasiek, warming to his work. With his saw he began cutting down exactly through the black penciled lines. When the piece was free, he laid it down upon another board and drew around it. Then he cut out a second piece exactly like the first.

"Whatever for?" Hanka whispered.

"For the cradle, of course," Jasiek said. "These are for end pieces. You wanted a rocking cradle, didn't you? Well then, watch." And with his hand he rocked the two rounding pieces. Now he planed them, rubbed them smooth, shaved off a bit with his sharp knife.

Hanka thought, "He is so slow. Why does he take so much time? The night will come down soon. Marta won't have a cradle tonight."

Jasiek answered her thoughts. "Even a doll's cradle, even a wooden toy, a horse or a man, even a spoon, must be perfect. Else the master craftsman down in the village would throw out the work." He bent lower. "That is where I'd like to go to school," he confessed in a whisper, "down in Zakopane, in the school for wood carvers."

Hanka opened wide her eyes. "You would leave us, Jas? You would not be a farmer like father? But how, then, could you carry on the farm for him?"

"Sh —" The boy wished he had not spoken at all. His face was flushed. "Of course I will carry on our farm, goosie. Would I ever want to leave home, leave our own highlands, our bit of a valley, our Polska? Except, of course, to see the world, other lands — just to see. But what's to prevent my becoming a wood carver, too? For the long winter evenings, when deep snow shuts us in?"

Hanka nodded, her eyes shining. For now she could see the cradle come alive in his hands. His long fingers were swiftly nailing the rounded head and footboards to the sides. Now he nailed slats across the bottom, and the cradle was done.

With a gasp of delight, Hanka ran to lift Marta from the box to the cradle. It was only a step, but what a difference it made! The size was perfect. The cradle rocked evenly and gently at the lightest touch of her hand. She laughed aloud.

"Oh, Jas, never any doll had so just-right a cradle as this."

"Ho, just you wait, now," said the boy. "It's not finished yet. Now watch!" On the headboard he drew a heart. On the footboard he drew three forget-me-nots with petals and leaves. The cradle he painted blue, like the robe of the Mother of God. The heart was red, and the blossoms were red, too, "because they are blushing like Marta's cheeks."

"Now it has only to dry," said the boy, surveying his work.

Hanka rushed about the big room to tell her mother making the soup, to tell Marysia bent over her sewing, to tell Burek dozing by the stove, to tell Babcia washing Zosia's face for supper.

"Come and see, come and see!" Hanka shouted as if they were deaf. "Jasiek has made such a cradle for Marta, the most lovely cradle that ever was made. Once it was a willow tree growing beside the brook. Once it made a cradle for bluebirds, and now it makes a cradle for Marta. And I shall keep it forever and ever, Amen."

⊰ 33 ⊱

All the family ran to see, even Father, who came in from feeding the stock.   Everyone talked at once.   Everyone admired the new cradle.

"A kind brother makes a kind father," said Babcia, smiling her wide, toothless smile at the boy.

Father took off his hat and scratched behind his ear. "We never know till we try, son, what our hands can do, if they are harnessed by the head, that is.   Well now, if you will take over the feeding and care of the new calf, perhaps she will bring enough at market to send you down to the woodworking school in Zakopane next year."

Jasiek was so happy he could not speak.   But Hanka ran to kiss her father's hand.   "It's all because Marta came to live with us," she cried.

CHAPTER 5

Of Dragons and Cradle Songs

NOW that Marta had a cradle of her very own, Hanka could put her down to sleep whenever she thought it good for her, just as Babcia did with Zosia. Mother and Marysia were often in the fields, now, helping to plant the good rye and the wheat. So the eldest and the youngest mothers kept house together.

But Hanka had a much easier job of it than Grandmother. For Zosia, just learning to walk and to talk, often refused to go to sleep. Instead, she kicked up her plump legs. She tossed her dimpled arms. First, she threw out her pillow. Next, she threw down her blanket to the floor.

Marta never did that. Marta did not cry. She was so good a child that her little mother had only to lay her down in the azure-blue cradle. At once her blue eyes closed. At once she fell fast asleep, while up in her cradle above, Zosia was still laughing or crying, or jabbering a talk all her own or screaming with wrath.

But even though Marta was so good, Hanka bent over the cradle a long time, rocking it gently forward and back, forward and back, singing to her that cradle song she loved the best. It was the same one that the Mother of God sang on Christmas Eve to her Babe.

Lullaby, little pearl,
dear baby Jezus,
Lullaby, little pearl,
dear baby sleeping.

And wonder of wonders, as Hanka sang to her doll, Zosia's long fringed lashes drooped, too. Soon she stopped kicking and squirming and throwing her arms about. She sighed, and turned her head on the pillow.

Grandmother smiled down at Hanka, as she pulled the cradle-cord backward and forward, forward and back. Hanka sang on :

OF DRAGONS AND CRADLE SONGS

Lullaby, Little One,
dear baby Jezus,
Mary is holding you,
guarding and keeping.

Marta was fast asleep. Singing to Marta, Hanka lulled
Zosia to sleep, too. Babcia was relieved. She put a finger
to her lips. Hanka nodded, gave a last pat to her small
cradle, brushed her lips across the smooth cheek. Then she
slipped off her shoes, and barefoot, like Babcia, they both sat
down on the bench just outside the door in the warm spring
sun.

"Tell me a story, Babcia dear," Hanka begged. "Please
do."

"Which one then, which shall it be?"

"About dragons, Babcia. About our own dragon, and
Jan."

So Grandmother began:

Once on a time, there lived in Poland a good man and his
good wife. Though they had a little farm, a horse and a
cow, a stork's nest on the barn, a cuckoo's nest in the alder
tree, they had no child. That was a grief to them: no
daughter, no son.

Now one night a storm blew down from the mountains,
with wind and thunder and rain. They heard a knocking
at the door. There stood a traveler, an old man with a long
white beard.

"May Pan Jezus be praised," said the man.   He asked for shelter.

"Forever and ever," they answered him.   They bade him come in.   They welcomed him in the name of the Lord. They gave him a seat by the fire to dry his coat.   They gave him a bowl of hot soup.   They gave him their bed.   More they could not do.

Early the next morning, as the stranger went on his way, he laid in the good wife's hand a white pearl.   He thanked them both for their kindness and said, "Now you shall have your dearest wish, yes, even a son who will be a great hero. You must call him Jan, Jan Perlowicz."

His words came true.   They had a son, and they named him Jan, Jan Perlowicz — John of the Pearl.   Now little Jan used to climb the paths through the Deep Forest into the hills above his home.   For here, in a log hut, lived an old hermit with a long white beard.   Yes, the same old man, the very same.   Jan loved the hermit and the hermit loved Jan.

One day he asked Jan, "Tell me, boy, what is the very worst and wickedest thing in all this world?"

Jan said, "The very worst and wickedest thing in the world is the terrible dragon that lives on the Tatra mountain peaks."

"Why so?" asked the hermit.

"Because he eats young girls, pretty girls with fair hair and blue eyes.   My mother told me so."

"Hum," said the hermit. "What a pity that there is no boy and no man strong enough and brave enough to slay that dragon, and so save all those pretty young maidens."

Jan jumped to his feet. "I will be that boy, and that strong man."

The hermit nodded his head. "Then you must do as I tell you to do. Each day you must pick up the largest stone you can lift and throw it from you."

Jan tried. Every day he lifted a stone, small at first, then larger and larger stones. Next he lifted a log. Soon he could uproot trees and fling them a long way. All this while Jan helped his father to plow, to reap, to thresh. He laughed because he grew as strong as his father, then stronger.

When he grew to young manhood, he told his hermit friend that now he must climb up to the peaks to try his luck at slaying the dragon.

"You will need more than luck, my son. Are you quite certain as yet of your strength? That dragon is a huge monster. I should have given you a few more years to prepare."

But Jan could not wait. So the old man blessed him, and away he strode.

At first the mountains were covered with mist, so Jan had to climb up and up before he caught sight of the dragon coiled around the Red Peaks, its head on one peak, its green scaly body trailing across the mountaintops.

Jan stood still in astonishment. He said to himself,

"That dragon is bigger than I thought. I must grow stronger, yet. The hermit is right."

So Jan worked at lifting more stones. For men he built houses, a stout house in a day. He made bridges and roads. And at last he made for himself a massive club with a head of stone. Then he climbed again up the Tatra peaks.

"Hi, ji, now, dragon," he called. "Here comes Jan Perlowicz to slay you and free all the country from dread of you."

The dragon wakened from sleep. He looked down his nose.

"Little man," he roared, "you may think you are strong. But one huff of my breath will destroy you." He shook with laughter.

Out blew a puff of white and poisonous vapor.

Jan jumped aside. Lifting a huge stone, a boulder, he hurled it at the dragon's head. Its crash made the mountains ring. Then with his mighty club, Jan dealt such a blow that he clove in the dragon's skull. In terrible pain and rage, the dragon lashed out its long tail, but Jan sprang aside, now under, now over, now leaping this way and that. Each time that Jan hurled a boulder, the dragon grew weaker and weaker until it could no longer huff or puff out its poisonous breath. It wanted only to escape from that strong little man.

So, slithering down from the Red Peaks, blind with pain, the huge creature rushed into a cave below to hide.

Then Jan ran after him, threw in mighty rocks that filled up the cave entrance, so that the dragon could never more come out. So the terrible beast died where it lay, inside the cave. And there, all the gnomes of the mountains buried its bones.

So never again was a happy young girl sacrificed for its food. The whole country was saved from its dread. And the place where the dragon found its cave was called —

Grandmother paused.

"I know," cried Hanka. "The dragon's cave was our own Zakopane, down in the valley below."

"Why, so it is," Babcia agreed. "That is so. And though now it is filled with houses and churches and shops and markets and schools, it is still surrounded with the jagged Red Peaks where Jan found the dragon."

"Yes, he was good and brave, that Jan."

"So it is lucky for a girl to marry a boy called Jan," said Babcia. "That is, if he be bold as he is good, and good as he is brave."

"Well then," said Hanka. "When I grow up, I shall marry a hero called Jan. And I shall call my little girl Marta, and my little boy a second Jan. And always I shall sing them my Jezus cradle song."

CHAPTER 6

The Best Day of the Week

FOR Hanka, Sunday was the very best day of the week. Not because it was a rest day from work, nor yet a rest day from play. But Sunday had a very special air. Breakfast was merry. They were all together. Father need not rush off to the fields, nor Jasiek to school. Hanka could watch them all dressing for church in their very best clothes.

Sometimes, on special saints' days, they took her with them, but it was far, and she was still small.

In the afternoon, they might all go to visit a neighbor, or a neighbor might come to visit with them. Sunday was a happy, friendly day.

But of course this Sunday was a very special day. Today was Marya Day, the day belonging to God's mother. Hanka waked her doll early, so as not to miss anything. The blue eyes stared and stared. For there was Zosia riding high on her father's foot, her chubby arms held in his big hands. Her red mouth was open wide, shouting with laughter and jabbering nonsense without a good Polish word in it. Father bobbed her up and down, up and down, as if his slippered foot were a little horse.

Of course Hanka must try the same game with Marta. And though the doll made no sound, she seemed to be enjoying the ride almost as much as laughing Zosia.

After breakfast, Marta must be shown all the Sunday bests. Hanka explained to her that all the while they had been playing house yesterday in the castle spruce tree, Mother and Marysia had been busy cleaning and mending, washing and pressing. So now Father and Jasiek put on their tight white trousers of snowy woven goat's hair embroidered in gay designs of red and blue and yellow wools. And each one had a clean white cotton shirt, as white as a cloud. And over the shirt hung the white felt coat. No man in the mountains bothered to thrust his arms into the sleeves. No, the coat was thrown around the shoulders, and tied under the chin with a wide red ribbon.

This, Hanka thought gayest of all, for the ends blew back in the wind when they walked. Each had a small round black felt hat with a string of sea shells called cowries on a red band around the crown. And Jasiek's hat boasted a tall feather.

"Yes, Marta," Hanka explained, "that's the tail feather of a great free bird called an eagle. And Jas climbed up to the nest for it, high up the rocks, all by himself!"

"And the white eagle belongs to Polska because it flies on our Polish flag," Jasiek added, smiling. "Tell Marta about that."

Hanka told, and then they visited the ladies. As for Mother's skirt, and Marysia's, they were of soft wool, flowered in lovely designs, like a meadow in spring. Very full, over many stiff white petticoats, they swirled as they walked. Mother's sleeveless jacket was lined with sheep's wool, while Marysia's jacket was bright red. Each wore a flowered head shawl tied under the chin.

Oh, Hanka was justly proud of her family. Only Grandmother did not dress up. Dear Babcia must stay at home to mind the baby. And Zosia and Hanka and Marta did not dress up, either. But — why not? This was such a sunny May day. And besides, was it not a special saint's day — the day of the very Lady of Paradise herself?

Hanka pulled her mother's skirt. "Oh, little mother,

Marta was dressed for Sunday, too

Mamusia, since I am now so old, and since Marta has never once been to church, please may we go, too?"

Mother smiled. "Well then, did you teach your child a prayer to say?"

Hanka hung her head. She was ashamed. Her cheeks burned red as Marta's. She said in a low voice, "I will begin this very night to teach her the *Our Father.*"

But Mother's hand was laid on her head. "Hurry then, child — slip into your best dress with the new red jacket."

"I'll help her," said Marysia. "I am all ready. Come, Hanka, we must not keep Father waiting."

Father was lighting his pipe and getting out his best axe-stick with the long shaft, to use as a cane. For what high-lander walked to church or anywhere else without his axe-stick?

Jasiek was giving a last polish to his boots, the new ones bought down in Zakopane market.

"They will hurt, son," warned his mother.

But they were shining and new, greased with fat from the skillet. Jasiek thought that he would not mind a little hurt to his heel or his toe. It would be nothing to the warm pride in his heart. Hanka thought he looked slim and hand-some in his tight, white trousers above the new boots.

But now she, too, was ready. Hands and face scrubbed clean, even the ears. Flowered skirt like a little garden, and bright red jacket with little round bonnet to match. Best of all, in her arms was Marta dressed for Sunday, too.

Church over in the next valley was a long way for small feet. But Hanka, her hand held fast in her mother's, could not keep her feet from dancing round and around the grown-ups. Soon Jasiek took off his shoes to carry in his hand, and so did she. Mother and Marysia did the same. They would walk down in comfort and put on the shoes just outside the church door.

Hanka was so happy, skipping to church, that she had to sing. So they all sang together *On the mountain the wind blows wild.* Their gay shouting voices tumbled down the hills.

After the song, Hanka thought of all she would show to Marta. First, the big square tower holding up the bells. Hark, one could hear them now, pealing out a gay jangle. And after church was over, Hanka thought how her family would surely linger talking with this one and that, while she, Hanka, would stand holding her doll, with a wide circle of admiring children around her.

But now they could look over the last hill and down to the valley below. She showed Marta the great strong church which the highland men had helped to build. Of pine trees, they made it, from the little clearing cut away at the edge of the forest. All the people going along to church looked like walking flowers from a high Tatra meadow. And now they all put on their shoes, not without some wry faces. Then in they all trooped through the wide-open wooden doors, studded with wooden nails.

Hanka whispered to Marta that the dim beauty inside must look like heaven. It was all so solemn. The men in white looked as if the snow had drifted down from the peaks ; while the women were like a giant flower bed against the dark walls.

How mysterious was the whispering of the prayers ! Hanka whispered the *Our Father,* too, loud enough so that Marta could hear. Marta must he held up to see the Father priest in his rich embroidered robes, and the little boys in white lace carrying big wax candles with a sweet smell.

And when the organ played, when the people sang the hymns and chants, Hanka knew the angels must be leaning down out of Paradise.

During the sermon Hanka crept away inside her own thoughts, where it was busy, but still. She liked to think how each family of the parish lived by itself like a little separate island, but how on Sunday they all came together, and melted into God. She liked to say it to herself :

> *"All of us belong to Father and Mother,*
> *Babcia, Marysia, Jasiek and Zosia ;*
> *not forgetting Hanka and Marta, too.*
> *But now we belong to all these people,*
> *and all these people belong to God.*
> *All of us belong to Poland,*
> *and Poland belongs to God, too."*

Thinking this, first she felt very small, and then she felt very large, and very safe.

But now the service was over. The organ played. The bells rang out. All the people streamed outside to stand in the sun and talk with their friends. Father would discuss weather and the crops. Marysia found the older boys and girls, Jasiek his friends. And holding Marta high so as not to be crushed in the throng, Hanka soon found that, just as she had imagined, all the little girls came running to her.

All but Jadwiga, who was lame. Jadwiga had to drag one leg. She had never owned a doll. Her eyes grew big with longing. She stretched out her arms.

Hanka found herself holding out Marta. And she saw Jadwiga's arms hug the doll tight as she bent to plant a big kiss on the rosy cheeks.

"Let me hold her," cried one little girl.

"No, me, Hanka, you promised her to me."

"You 've had her long enough," said another, snatching her out of Jadwiga's arms.

Their excited voices sounded like the shrill chattering of magpies. Hanka frowned. It was not how she had seen it in her mind. After all, Marta was her doll, and now the girls were about to tear her apart with their longing hands. Already the bonnet was off, the dress unfastened, yes, even the petticoats, too, when they turned Marta upside down. Hanka was nearly in tears.

At that moment the Reverend Father came up. He smiled.

"Well now, what have we here ?" He himself gently lifted the doll. He straightened the dress ; he restored the bonnet. "Now tell me, who is your mother, little one ?" he asked the blue eyes.

"She can't talk Polish yet, Father," Hanka told him. "But when she can, she will know the *Our Father*, because I shall begin tonight to teach it to her. *Our Father, who art in Heaven*, that's how she will say it."

"And quite right, too. That's how all little mothers teach their children. No better mothers in all the world than ours in the Tatra. That's because the edges of Paradise rest here on the peaks of our own mountains."

He stroked the real hair. The children were silent, though all the bright eyes were fixed on the doll.

"Shall I speak her a little sermon ? You all know the proverb : *As the mother, so is the child.* It works both ways. Remember, that as you take care of your dolls, so you will one day take care of your own little ones."

"Yes, Father," said Hanka, her face shining. And all the others echoed her with soft voices, "Yes, Father."

"And now, always and for always, remember one thing more. From the Tatra peaks of our high Carpathian mountains to the faraway Baltic Sea, we are all children of one earth father-mother, the Polish Fatherland. And no matter

our faith or creed, we are all children of one heavenly mother
— the — "

But all the children shouted it before he could say it —
"The Queen of Heaven !"

"There ¡   You all know her better than I."   As, smiling,
he handed Marta back to her own little mother, the children
ran forward to kiss his hand.

Hanka heard her mother calling, "Come, Hanka, come
my child."

"Good-bye, little Father, dear," Hanka said.   "And
Marta says it too."

At home, when Hanka's tired feet had toiled all the long
way up the hills, her grandmother asked, "And did Marta
enjoy the church today, Hanka ?"

"Oh, yes, Babcia.   The Reverend Father spoke her a little
sermon, just for her.   Of course I must take good care of
her, because she is my baby.   I wouldn't want to carry my
own children upside down, nor leave them out in the rain,
now would I ?"

Babcia laughed.   "Or drop them into the hot ashes on
the hearth.   No, child, I expect you will be the best little
mother a doll may have, ever."

CHAPTER 7

Dancing with a Doll

NOW, whoever heard of a doll taking part in a dance and helping to put out a fire!"

That is what all the tongues said later, up and down the highlands. Marta grew so famous that she blushed and blushed again. This is how it happened.

Cousin Frania from over the mountains was to marry

Michal from two valleys below. They had met summers on the high pastures, tending their herds. They decided to set up a home together. Michal's father gave him the farm. Mother told it to Father and he to Babcia and she to Marysia and she to Jasiek and he to Hanka and she, of course, to Marta.

Before the wedding would come the dance of the *dobra nocka*, the wedding eve. The whole family was invited to come, riding in the cart with the horse. Yes, even little Zosia this time, and of course, Marta, too.

Hanka caught up her doll with a big hug. "And they say never you saw such dancing as there will be !"

It was true ; never she did. Seated on the floor, leaning against Babcia's knees, Hanka and Marta watched the dancing all the afternoon long. In Babcia's lap, Zosia had fallen asleep. But Marta must stay awake today, for who could sleep with so much to see ?

Hanka's own eyes were bright with excitement, her cheeks flushed a rosy red as she watched how the men danced together while the girls looked on. Now the girls danced together and the boys looked on. Now the girls danced with the boys and the boys with the girls. Hanka felt she could never look enough.

Nor could she listen enough. For it was the music, the gay, breathless Polish music that made everybody's heart jump so that they danced however the music was playing,

Marysia danced with her two girl friends

as if a spell had been put upon them all. As if they could not stop dancing.

When the boys danced the *bandit dance*, first the feet came together with a click, and then they sprang wide apart. Now the knees bent forward, now the legs leapt up tall and straight. Now the hands clapped, now the feet pounded the floor. Hanka could feel the boards shake, and the shake went up her spine.

All the watchers clapped hands or stamped gaily to the throb of the violins, basses, accordions and flutes. Soon Hanka was keeping time to a polka. One, two, three, *hop*; one, two, three, *whirl*. She tapped with Marta's arm, so as to teach Marta the rhythm, too. Mothers tapped their feet, or nodded their heads. In Hanka's head, the dance music made words and sang a tune.

"Baby Zosia is asleep. She is too little to dance. Marta and I will whirl and whirl, round and round like a spinning top, with the tune in our feet and a song in our head."

Hanka jumped to her feet. She would go to dance with the grown-ups. But Babcia pulled her back. She was still too small. "Only watch, watch your pretty big sister, now."

When Marysia danced with her two girl friends, the full skirts billowed out wide, bright kerchiefs fell back from their shining faces. Ah, yes, the musicians knew well how to make the young feet fly, because some of the fiddlers were gypsies !

Now just as Hanka was whispering that to her doll, things

began to happen to that small person. The bridegroom Michal, who was to wed Cousin Frania from over the mountains, was dancing a solo *mazur* for his bride. He came leaping, whirling, flying across the floor, but stopped short almost at Hanka's feet. He bent and clapped his hand on the floor.

Hanka thought he must be going to leap over her head, but instead, seeing the doll in her arms, a sudden whim made him catch up Marta and go whirling away with her. The bride Frania laughed. All the girls laughed, all the mothers, all the boys and the men. For Michal began doing funny sweet things with Marta in *mazurkas*, — little dances all his own. Now he tossed up the doll on high, and he caught her again. He threw her now under the right leg, now under the left. And all in time to the music.

Hanka gasped, her mouth open, her hands clasped, half in terror, lest Marta fall, half in delight. But now the other boys joined in the fun, and some of the older girls, too. Marta was tossed gaily from one side to another. And as the music went faster and faster, so went the dance, until the poor thing was in danger of losing her breath altogether, and Hanka's with her.

For at that moment, Michal caught the doll away from his bride and threw her hard across the room. But instead of being caught by one of the dancers, Marta crashed right through the windowpane and outside the house. Michal gave a running leap through the window after her.

Then Hanka got to her feet, and ran, too. If only she could once more clasp Marta safe in her arms, she would never let them have her again, never. Hanka leaned out the broken window.

Outside, Michal was searching about the ground underneath. "Have any of you seen a doll go dancing off down the hill?" he asked of the men lounging on the bench outside, getting a bit of fresh air, and catching their breath.

"She's gone riding off down the hill, all right," one of them replied, laughing. "For she landed right in the middle of neighbor Stas' cart. He's driven off down yonder to feed his stock. He'll soon return."

Hanka, listening, put both hands over her mouth. Marta gone! Riding off alone downhill in a cart. She called to Michal:

"Save her, cousin, save her. She'll be sure to jolt out somewhere on the road."

"Hi, ji, little mother, we'll soon have your child back again," he answered. "Come on, all you inside who are ready to go forth to rescue a damsel — lest a terrible dragon consume her."

Laughing, shouting, a crowd of older boys and girls ran out through the door, Marysia among them. When she saw that Hanka ran, too, she took the child's hand.

"Don't fret, Hanka. Michal will soon find her. He would never let harm come to your Marta. You know the dragon is just for pretend."

Some turned back. Why leave a dance for a doll! Neighbor Stas would soon be driving back up the hill again. But the rest ran on. So they had a great race down the hill after the cart. And though Hanka's feet were the very smallest of them all, she kept up with the rest. Her heart was pounding, and her eyes prickled between laughter and tears.

Now neighbor Stas had a good swift little horse, so he was already turning into his own barnyard when they caught up.

But what was that shooting up behind the house? Flames, red flames against the sunset sky. His barn was on fire! And no one left at home to do anything about it, since the wife and daughter and small sons were all up at the dance. Now they all heard the cows lowing in fright, the pigs squealing, the sheep bleating, the hens clucking, the geese squawking; and no one to drive them to safety.

But now, thanks to Marta, there was help. Marta and Hanka were both forgotten as the men rushed to the rescue. Michal, with an axe, mounted a ladder to chop away the burning roof. Of wooden shingles it was, dry as a boiled bone. The girls must form a brigade of buckets from the spring. The boys threw the water on the blaze. Luckily, there was no wind. Fortunately, too, neighbor Stas was just in time to lead out the poor frightened beasts, to herd them all into the dark cowshed on the other side of the house. Then he rushed back to direct the fire fighters.

And where was Hanka? Seeing, like a sensible child,

that she was really too small to help, and might only get in the way, she climbed up into the four-wheeled cart. On her hands and knees she searched in the straw on the floor till she found an object. Minus a bonnet, with fine hair all tangled, with dress and petticoats crumpled, yet it was still Marta, safe again, in her own arms once more. Hanka held her close, close. And she planted a big kiss on the rosy cheeks as she crouched there in the straw.

Hanka choked with the strong acrid smell of smoke. In her ears she heard a chorus of smothered cries from the dumb frightened beasts; of moos and squawks and baas and neighs. She thrust the doll inside her jacket with only the head and arms sticking out. Then the little girl ran to comfort the beasts. She pushed inside the small shed among them.

"There, *Pani* Cow — Mrs. Cow, don't take on so. See, the fire did not burn you. Here, I'll bring you your calf. Sh, dear, here, have a handful of hay to eat."

Marta looked on with wide-open blue eyes, while Hanka petted the stamping snorting horses, and soothed the pigs. She gathered the chicks about their mother and shooed the clucking cocks from underfoot into a far corner by themselves.

And all the while, she talked to them as if they were people like you and like me. She told them about Pan Jezus and his mother Marya, Mary, the Queen of Heaven, the Lady of Poland.

"She would not let the fire burn you, sillies," Hanka told all the creatures. "She has eyes like the stars ; never she sleeps at all."

Now whether the beasts really understood her words, since it was not yet Christmas Eve, at least they took great comfort from her voice. They crowded about her, munching from a manger the hay she kept bringing them to eat. So gradually the moos, the baas, the squawks, the cluckings, the snortings ceased. They stood close together, waiting patiently. They even dozed a bit, or munched hay in content.

Then, because she was very tired, and the place was smelly and warm and dark, Hanka climbed up into the manger herself. And there it was that, when the fire was all put out, Michal and neighbor Stas found her when they came with a lantern. Hanka was fast asleep in the manger, with Marta held fast in her arms.

So Michal carried them both back up the hill in his strong young arms. Hanka was glad because she could show Marta the stars. For the first time in Marta's life, she saw the planet Jupiter, and Venus blazing like a lamp in the east. And overhead the great Milky Way was stretching across the sky — the way where the Heavenly Queen walks at night.

And though, after that adventure, the young people danced on right through the night until the dawn, Hanka and Marta did not stay awake to see. For the music sang them to sleep. And in Hanka's dreams, she saw all the stars in the night sky dancing together.

So that is how the story of Marta traveled up hill and down, because of course no one in the Tatra had ever before owned a doll who took part in a wedding-eve dance and who helped to put out a fire.

CHAPTER 8

Which Is Best?

THE next week, who should come to pay them a visit but Grandfather from two mountains above. Hanka saw him striding along the road, thin and straight. She and Marta ran to meet him.

"May the Lord be praised," said Grandfather, opening wide his arms. "And how goes my little Hanka?"

"For ever and ever," cried Hanka, running into his arms.

"And oh, Dziadek — Grandfather dear, Marta and I are glad to see you."

"Well, now, so this is Marta! What a famous dancer she has become! All the highland lads are singing her praises."

Hanka beamed. She saw that he carried on his back his bagpipe, shaped like a little goat. That was a better gift than a sweet in his pocket, for now he would make music all the day.

As he greeted the family, as he ate his bread and cheese, Hanka kept as close to him as his shadow. She followed him out to the barnyard where he sat down on a bench near the cowshed. Of course his bagpipe went with him. She watched him fit the mouthpiece into the left corner of his smiling, toothless mouth, and finger the stops. When the first quavering notes began to swirl out the tune, Hanka jumped to her feet.

"I know, it's a polka, Grandfather. It's the very same tune they played at the wedding-eve dance."

He nodded, a pleased smile lighting his face and playing among the brown wrinkles. With his hands he motioned to her to begin. One, two, three, *hop*; one, two, three, *whirl*.

So Hanka began to spin in circles, round and round. No one to tell her now, "You are too small." Since Marta liked to dance, too, they faced each other, hand in hand. Together they whirled round and around. Now feet together, now wide apart, Hanka followed the music, just as she had seen the grown-ups at the big dance.

And just as Hanka's feet went, so went Marta's. She was light as a fairy, her small feet hardly touching the ground.

"Wonderful!" cried Grandfather, pausing for breath. "Only wait a bit, Hanka, to grow tall. You will have all the boys running after you to dance with them. Soon you will dance with the best in the parish. Only feel the music, and your feet will dance of themselves."

Hanka's face shone like a round sun. She felt very happy. Something in the motion, the whirling, the keeping time to the swirling tune made her happy deep inside her heart.

"He means that he thinks Marta was doing well, too," she thought. "For how could I dance without her? And now Marta knows the dance better than I do."

When they were tired, they dropped down beside Grandfather for a story. He knew so many stories. That one about Jan Perlowicz slaying the dragon. All the ones about robber Janosik and his merry band of bandits.

The day was still. A lark was trilling high in the blue above their heads. Some pigeons were crooning under the low eaves. Burek barked, chasing the hens. Now he came panting to lie down at their feet.

"If you tell us an animal story, Dziadek dear, then Burek will listen, too."

"Well then," said Grandfather, half shutting his eyes,

Together they whirled round and around

"how would you like the story of the night when **Pan Jezus** was born ?"

"Oh, yes, tell us that one," Hanka agreed.

So Grandfather began.

Before ever the angels had told the shepherds tending their flocks on the hills, before ever the star had led the three Kings from the East, the animals all came to hail Pan Jezus as king.

Only later, when shepherds and kings and countryfolk, too, had crowded the dumb beasts out of the shed, the animals stood all together having their say. Each wanted to be first in importance that glad night.

The ox and the ass said, "We are best because we warmed the Babe with our breath."

The sheep quickly said, "But we are best because we gave the Child the wool from our backs to make Him a coat."

The cow said, "But I am best, next to His mother, because I gave Him my milk to drink."

The billy goat said, "But I it is who am best because with my thick head, with my horns, I butted away the wolf who would have eaten the Child."

"How you misjudge me," said the wolf. "I'd not harm a hair of His head. You've no occasion to show off like that. I'm best myself because I carried the little dear my own dinner, a silly lamb that had strayed from the fold."

The big bear said, "Who's best but me ? I am best. I

brought fresh honey from the forest. Mother Mary will strain it, golden and sweet; honey fit for the Prince of Peace." The big fellow stood up on his hind legs, licking his lips with his long red tongue.

Now a sheep dog bounded among them. "If there's talk of the best, it is I. Who else guarded the sheep while all the shepherds ran to adore?"

But who could decide which was best? Just then, they heard Pan Jezus calling in a voice like a chime of bells. It was deep night and the world was asleep. The shepherds slept by their sheep. The three Kings slept, and their pages and camels, too. Only the stars still sang together, but so high and faraway the song, that men could not hear.

When the animals all drew near the manger, they saw the Christ Child sitting up in the hay, His left hand in His mother's who slept by His side. At His feet lay a lamb. In His right hand they all saw a bird, a small field lark, with bright beady black eyes.

The Child smiled under His golden curls. Gently slipping His left hand from His mother's, He motioned them near.

"You've been wondering, brothers dear, which of you is the best?"

"That's right, sweet Prince. Who else should tell us?"

"Well then, I thank you, ox, and you, ass, for warming me with your breath. I thank you, sheep, for the warm wooly coat. And you, Pani cow, for your sweet white milk. And

Billy Goat dear, thanks for protecting me. Though brother wolf was quite right, he really would not have hurt a hair of my head. So thanks to you, wolf, for the gift of your lamb. And you, big bear, for the sweet golden honey. I suppose you really can't help stealing a bit from the bees, now and then. And you, good dog, my thanks for guarding the sheep so your masters could come down from the hills. They all pledged allegiance. They gave me their hearts."

Pleased with themselves, glad of the heart-warming praise, all the animals crowded still closer. The little lamb, seeing them, shrank down in the hay and trembled on its wobbly legs, until the Lord Jezus stroked its wooly head.

"But see here, my friends." Pan Jezus held up his right hand still holding the bird, the little field lark. "While you all gave me fine gifts, the lark gave me only herself. Yes, she came fluttering into my hand and she sang:

" 'Sweetest Lord Jezus, I am not much to see, being only the color of earth. But my bright eyes are yours, my free wings are yours, and so is my song. So take me, all of me, just as I am.'

"Now which gift, do you think, is the best?"

The ox and the ass hung their heads. They looked away from the Child. So did the sheep, and the wolf and the cow, the goat and the dog. As for the big bear, he swung his head from side to side, and he could not help taking just a lick or two of the honey still in the honeycomb! But he agreed with the others. All the animals said it together:

"Yes, it is so, Pan Jezus, little dove. Though that lark is not much to look at, though she is so small, and only the color of earth, still she is best. She has given you most. She gave her bright eyes, her free wings and her song. She gave you herself, what there was of her."

And that is why, to this very day, of all the creatures on earth, or above the earth, or beneath ; of them all, the lark's song is sweetest and best.

Grandfather was silent. Hanka and Marta and Burek were silent, too. For high overhead, in the warm stillness, they heard a song, thrilling and gay, out of the heart of a lark.

"I suppose she still sings to Pan Jezus," Hanka whispered. "I suppose she flies back and forth between earth and heaven to carry the news of men to Our Lady. And when she flies back she sings all the news of Paradise."

Grandfather nodded. "When we peasants reap the wheat, if we find a lark's nest, we leave a patch of grain growing around it, so the nest is undisturbed. For Pan Jezus' mother walks down from the Milky Way to protect her lark."

That night at supper, Hanka asked, "Little Mother, Mamusia, which of your children is best ? Which of us do you love the most ?"

Jasiek answered quickly. "That's easy. She loves Marysia most because she helps most."

Marysia said quickly, "But surely both parents love you most, Jas. You chop the wood for the stove. You help in the fields. In summer, you mind the herds on high pastures. One day, Father will leave this whole farm to you."

Babcia smiled a sly smile. "But perhaps now, they love Zosia best because she is the smallest, the most like an angel."

Hanka could not help saying quickly, "And perhaps they even love Marta best, because she is so obedient. She never cries, and she is so very small."

Across the table, across the empty soup bowl, Mother and Father looked at each other. They smiled. They looked at Grandfather, at Father's father. They looked at Grandmother, at Mother's mother. At each they smiled.

Hanka went to stand beside her mother, pressing against her, with Marta held in her arms.

"Mother, you didn't say. You only smiled. Tell it then, which is the most important of us all. Which one do you love the most?"

"Now go along with you, child." Mother laughed. "You should know, all of you, that I love you each the same. And I could not love any of you more. So there!" She wiped her eyes on her apron.

Father added, "No one is greatest among you, or most important of all. Each fills his own place, like the fingers of my hand. Without each one what should any of us do? How have a home without your mother? How should I manage the farm and the stock without Jasiek and Marysia? What would Babcia do without Zosia, or Hanka without her Marta?"

"Yes," Hanka said to her doll. "They all love you, and when Marysia is married, you shall dance at her wedding, too."

Jasiek shouted. "Only wait till Marysia finds her a beau."

Marysia blushed and tousled his hair.

So then Jasiek got out his flute and Father his fiddle and Grandfather his bagpipe. And they played a gay tune, a lively Polish air. And Hanka danced with Marta, and Mother with Marysia and Babcia with Zosia. And a shining light glowed in all their faces, a light of happiness in their hearts.

Each had his place and all belonged together. As Father said:

"As a family, together we stand or fall. However good and brave is each of us, and honest, so also is the family. And just so, however brave and honest each family, so goes all Poland. We stand or fall with our nation. She stands or falls with us."

"Well then," said Jasiek, "if that is so, I think our family will not just stand. We will march forward!"

CHAPTER 9

High Pastures

EVER since the day Marta came to live with Hanka, three days before the name day of her Saint Anna, they had done exciting things. Together they had been to church, together they had learned to dance.

One summer day, Hanka heard her mother say to Marysia, "Already up there on the high pastures, on the *hala* where Jasiek minds the herds, the nights will be cold. He will be wanting another warm coat, a woolen cloth to bind about his feet. See, I have baked him some fresh *kolacz*. Would you like to walk up to him tomorrow?"

Hanka's heart skipped faster.   She ran to the small blue cradle.

"Wake up, wake up, Marta.   Marysia is going to carry some things up to Jas.   And, oh, how I wish we could go, too."

She gathered up her doll and tiptoed to her mother's side. She stood very close against her, like a cat that begs for its milk.

Mother's hands were busy putting things into a basket : a roll of sausage, a mound of *kolacz* — small round sweet buns filled with prune jam.   She gave Hanka a little push.

"There now, child, run and play."

But Hanka pressed closer.   She even buried her face in her mother's apron.   "But I am no longer a child," she whispered.   "I am a little mother.   You yourself often say it. Marta wants so much to go, too.   And so do I.   Else who would carry her ?"

Mother laughed.   Marysia laughed.

"Well then, why not let her go ?" Marysia asked.   "If the little mother can walk all the road to church and back, dancing down the whole way, why not up to visit Jasiek ?   He and the lambs will be glad to see her.   And Burek will be wild with delight."

"Oh, yes, Mamusia dear, please do say that we may go. Marta shall wear the new dress that Cousin Frania made her after the big dance."

"You won't get too tired, then ?" asked her mother.

"You won't ask Marysia to carry you ? You'll obey her like a sensible child ?"

Hanka promised. She promised all three. Her heart danced. She had to run out to the castle to tell the spruce tree. She must tell the hens, the ducks, the geese, the pigs. She ran to tell her father the moment he came from the fields to milk the cows. Beautiful, wonderful news !

Next day, they started soon after dawn, with the sun just touching the mountaintops to reddish gold. The road led out and up from their valley into the wide world. Now Hanka must not dance ; she must walk. For the road was very long and led up very high, her sister said. Jasiek's *hala*, his mountain pasture, was up there among the peaks, quite out of sight. That was why they must walk on and on one hour, two hours, three, four. When her shoes pinched, Hanka took them off. When the stones hurt her feet, she put on her slippers. When her feet ached more, she told them not to mind.

As they went on up, Hanka understood many new things about the mountains heard in songs, in stories told by Grandfather and Jasiek.

She shivered as they entered into the Deep Forest of red pine. Inside, it was dim, almost dark, mysterious, like church. The high branches overhead shut out the blue sky. They made a sobbing sound like the organ. Hanka held Marta closer. Surely there were gnomes and fairies hiding here, and wild creatures, too. Perhaps a wolf, or a huge black bear. Once she caught sight of a wild doe, standing as still as a breath.

Marysia searched for the blossoming fern, even though it was not midnight, not June. "Because whoever finds the fern in bloom will see all the treasures of earth, above or beneath," she told her small sister in a whisper.

Hanka took a long deep breath when at last they came safely out of the Deep Forest into an open meadow bright with green grass and sunshine.

Once, when they climbed a rocky path to the top of the world, Marysia said, "Look back, look back down. There below lies Zakopane, there in the old dragon's cave."

Hanka looked. So that was Zakopane, their own market town, their very own. Never had she seen it before.

"Why!" she gasped. "It is no bigger than a doll city! The houses and the churches are so small that even Marta would feel at home in them. I suppose the people have now turned into little black ants."

Only the mountains were vast, the great jagged Red Peaks powdered with snow. Marysia pointed. "That one is Giewont, the sleeping knight. See, he stands guard over Zakopane with the cross on his shield."

Hanka saw. She looked with all her eyes. And she pointed it out to Marta. The peaks where lived the dragon slain by Jan. The river that looked like a shining thread; the lakes reflecting the sun.

Then they trudged on and on. Hanka was warm, then hot. So she slipped off her head shawl, she tied her warm coat around her waist. Still, they trudged on.

When they came to a big blackberry patch, Marysia said, "Here let us stop for a rest." For who could walk past such berries as these? Marysia put down her heavy basket, which she had balanced on a stick over her shoulder. On the basket Hanka laid Marta for a bit of a nap. Then they picked and they picked, filling their mouths with the big ripe berries, sweeter and bigger than any Hanka had tasted in the thickets near home. When they had eaten their fill, Hanka looked at her sister and laughed.

"You have a purple face!"

"So have you."

They were glad of a mountain brook close by. Flat on her stomach, Hanka buried her face in the water. She drank and drank. She washed her face and hands. If only she could lie down and sleep! But they must be up and away. The path was no more than a cow trail, rocky and steep. Marysia pushed from behind. For Hanka was panting for breath in the thin high air.

"Is it much farther? When shall we ever arrive?" She asked it again and again.

"Only a little way, now. See, we've climbed above tree line. Only dwarf pines and junipers now. Over this spur we climb, that's a big girl. Now, look!"

Hanka looked. She cried out with joy. On the high open slope were pink grasses and a carpet of wild flowers. She longed to lie down and roll, then to pick and pick.

"Here are blue gentians," she cried, "and scarlet poppies, and red columbine, and tall Queen Anne's lace, and small white saxifrage and pinks. Here is every flower that blooms, all together, all at once."

"Yes," Marysia agreed. "Here it's like Heaven. I always think I may meet her here — that Lady of Paradise — walking here among the flowers, with the sweet breath of the snowy peaks blowing her hair."

Hanka nodded her head. "Oh, Marysia, let's stay here all the day."

But Marysia pointed above them, higher still. What! could it be the *hala* at last? Hanka could see the roofs of the log huts for the shepherds. So, they had almost arrived. Now as they climbed, they heard the sound of the long trumpets, calling the sheep. And soon their ears caught the tinkle of bells, sheep bells, cow bells. And at last they were walking among the flocks. Marysia's calls, her wave, Hanka's shouts were answered with happy calls echoing and reëchoing.

"Even the mountains are glad we have come," Hanka gasped, out of breath.

Now Jasiek saw them, and came running down the hill with Burek at his side. The dog bounded forward to meet them. In his joy he knocked Hanka down. Marta fell down, too. The dog would have shaken the breath out of the poor doll if Jasiek had not rescued her. The boy shouted, "*Ai, ji, ji !*"

He kissed his sisters on both cheeks. Yes, he even kissed Marta too. She cuddled down in his big pocket where he thrust her.

Proudly, he began pointing out his sheep. How the lambs had grown ! Hanka began chasing them as if she had not just climbed for four hours up the long trail. The lambs knew her and licked her face. Then they must meet Marta and lick her pink cheeks.

Everyone was enormously happy. Burek, perhaps, most of all.

"See," said Hanka, "Burek is both laughing and crying for joy." She threw her arms around his big body, mindful of the spiked collar he wore around his neck up here in the heights, lest a wolf come at night after the sheep.

While Marysia ran off to visit her friends keeping their flocks, Hanka sat down on a big rock beside her brother. She was soon shivering in the high sharp wind, blown down from the snowy peaks towering above them. She was glad of her warm shawl and coat. Jasiek was glad of his warm new sheepskin coat. He played for Hanka on his flute, the willow pipe he had made.

Little shepherd, to the meadow do not lead your sheep.

While he played the highland airs, wild and sweet, Burek

lay stretched at Hanka's feet, his head in her lap. The lambs skipped about her. Again they must kiss Marta and admire her new dress.

Now a trumpet call sounded, and soon all together, with the *baca,* the old head shepherd, the boys and girls crowded into one of the huts to eat their bread and cheese, the good cheese made from sheep's milk. They drank their big mugs of milk. Jasiek opened his basket. He shared his sausage and all his jam cakes, every one. The tongues wagged fast. Marysia must tell them of all that had happened in the parish down below. Hanka showed them her doll. She told them Grandfather's story of the animals and Pan Jezus. Then they must sing a song and dance a shepherd's dance, all together, Marysia and Hanka, too.

If only the sun would stand still! But all the while he was slipping down the mountainsides. Before they knew it, the peaks were turning from a white glory to shell pink. Then Marysia must tear herself away.

"Come, Hanka, we must hurry home, before darkness catches us, down in the Deep Wood."

So over and over they all said good-byes. Across the wide *hala* they called back and forth. The boys blew into their long wooden trumpets until the poor sheep came running this way and that, at the booming sound.

"Tell Mother, thanks for the *kolacz,*" Jasiek called.

So in all the merry cries and messages and sounds, down

the long slope of wildflowers Marysia and Hanka ran, pell mell, laughing, with Burek leaping and bounding beside them, trying to snatch Marta's foot. At last Marysia must send him back. For already the rocks had begun, the sharp path that took so long to climb, but was so easy to run down.

Only Hanka's toes pushed too far forward in her shoes. But she had to wear them for the jagged stones.

Would they reach the Deep Forest before dark? Would a dragon lurk there to devour them? Or a gray wolf or a big black bear? As they entered, Hanka shivered with dread. Marysia took her hand. The very stillness hurt her ears. She started as a deer went bounding out of a fern thicket, as frightened as she. The hanging lichens had faces. Behind the fallen logs lurked — who could say?

Then at last they came out of the Deep Forest to the top of the world. They looked down upon Zakopane, already glowing with a thousand, ten thousand little lights.

"Like a flock of stars fallen into the big dragon's cave," Hanka said.

After that, who could be afraid, even though the twilight was fast coming upon them. So they ran and they ran, on and on, down the path and into the road, the road to the wide world that led them back home.

Home! How good to see their own yellow lamplight. How sweet and rosy was Zosia's face, and how kind Babcia's eyes. How warm and soft were Mother's arms as Hanka ran to press her face against them. How delicious the smell of the soup bubbling on the stove, and how fragrant the smoke from Father's pipe.

When Hanka and Marysia had told all there was to tell, there remained one thing more.

"Yes," sighed Hanka, forgetting about her swollen feet. "This has been surely the best day of my life, and Marta says so, too. Because now we are growing big enough to climb our mountains. There the sheep and Burek and Jas and the winds are *free* !"

Father took out his pipe. He nodded to Mother. He scratched behind his ear. A broad smile spread over his long face.

"There ! The child is one of us. She has caught it on her very first climb. The word that we highlanders learn on the high pastures, the word blown down from our high peaks."

"What word, Father ?" Hanka was curious.

"The word shouted by the white eagle on our red flag — *Freedom.* Never forget, little Hanka, that word spells *Poland.*"

CHAPTER 10

The Bandit of Bandits

IN another month, Jasiek came down from the mountains, driving his cows and his sheep. The whole family were glad to welcome them.

"The Lord be praised!" said Mother. "You 've grown nearly as tall as a man, son."

"For ages and ages," said Jasiek smiling. "For all the free life on the heights, a man likes to come home."

Already, up there, snow had fallen. "It will be an early winter, Father, they say." And Father nodded his head.

Hanka remembered how, last winter, she had to stay indoors for long weeks, pressing her nose to the cold frosty windowpane. The snow was too deep. She was too little for the drifts, her mother said. The cold was too sharp.

But now she had Marta. The winter world would be different this year, as the summer had been.

When, in late November, winter tumbled down from the mountains, when the snows shut her in, Hanka played endless games with Marta of "I am the mother, you are my little girl," or "I am the teacher, you are my pupil."

Then Grandfather came more and more often to stay. Hanka at the window saw him come. "Look, Marta, there comes our Dziadek with his bagpipe on his back. And what do you think he brings us in his pockets this time?"

Marta could not guess. So they ran to meet him, stamping in the dark entryway, brushing off the dry snow. Even little Zosia toddled to greet him. She, too, had learned to expect a gift.

So the three smallest ones danced around him. Would it be candy wrapped in gay papers? Or a gingerbread man?

Grandfather smiled and slowly put his hand into his right pocket. No, nothing there. The hand came out empty. Into his left pocket, then. No, nothing there, either.

"Look inside!" Hanka shouted.

"Ah, yes, something may just be hiding inside." And out it came — a big crusty crescent covered with poppy seeds.

Now the bagpipe made the big room gay with dancing.

Hanka and Marta practiced all the steps, the quick one, two, three, *hop*, of the polka, the lively mazurka in three-eighth or three-quarter time.   She danced till she was tired and dropped down on her own red bench to listen.   The warm stove, the soft music made her eyes droop.

But the moment her grandfather began to tell a story, that was different.   Then she must rub her eyes wide awake. And hold up Marta, too, so as not to miss a word.   Of course she never tired of animal stories, nor the one about the dragon of Zakopane.   But Jasiek always begged for tales of the bold brave bandit Janosik.

Then all the family listened, too.   Mother looked over her mending, Father over his carving, and Marysia over her embroidery.   Silently, without a lullaby, Babcia rocked Zosia to sleep.   But Jasiek came to sit down at Grandfather's feet while he whittled a wooden toy.   Hanka and Marta leaned against his bench.   For who in all the land did not love to hear the stories of Janosik, the mountain bandit of long ago ?

"Begin when he was a boy," Hanka begged.   "Begin where he was lost in crossing through the Deep Forest." Now it came to her that for the first time, since her journey up to the high pastures, she knew how he felt, that robber boy lost in the wood.

So Grandfather began.

Once on a time in our land, long ago, when Polish nobles

had more power and riches than goodness of heart, when for the poor there was scant justice in the land, there grew up a highland boy called Janosik.

Well then, when the boy lost his way in the woods, he was not frightened by the great trees, by the bear and the wolf. His heart was as bold and as brave as theirs. So they respected him and even showed him the way to a small house in a clearing, the home of three witches.

Out of the door popped one old head, two old heads, three. They looked at the boy and nodded. "It is he."

The first witch set the boy to splitting wood with a dull axe. He set his teeth and he worked till he had a neat pile.

The second witch set Janosik at weaving white cloth on a loom. She showed him how to throw the shuttle now over, now under the warp. The boy did his best.

The third witch set the boy at tanning leather. It had a bad smell. But Jan took a deep breath and rubbed the stretched hide with a stone.

The witches were well pleased. Next day before setting him on his way, each gave him a gift. The first gave him a magic stick-axe. He had only to lean upon it like a cane and make a wish. With the swiftness of wind it would carry him over the earth.

The second witch gave the boy a white shirt which no bullet, no blade could pierce.

The third witch's gift was a leather belt which gave him the strength of ten.

They danced in high hats, stick-axes in hand

Each one said, "Janosik, go forth and become the world's boldest bandit, of robbers the king. But mind, only for a good cause, only to bring justice back to our land."

Now when the boy Janosik grew to manhood, he gathered about him a band of like men, with courage and daring in their hearts, with strength and boldness in their arms. Oh, it was not easy to become a member of that band. The entrance trial was a hard one. A youth must be able to leap over a burning fire, at the same moment with one hand shooting with his pistol the top of a pine, and with the other hand cutting off the plume of another tree with his curved knife.

But, once accepted, they obeyed the law of each for all and all for each. They righted all wrongs. They gathered in the riches of greedy men to feed the poor and those forced to work without wage.

So they roamed our hills like the eagles, bold and free, a cave for their fortress and home. They danced the bandit dance in high hats, with stick-axes in hand. When they were not robbing, they danced and fiddled and sang. The peasants loved them, but wicked men hated and feared them, because the leader Jan led a charmed life. With his axe, his white shirt and his belt who could harm him ? Who could take revenge ? So his fame spread to peasant and nobleman till it reached the ears of the king.

Now in those days there came an army invading Poland, led by a German emperor come to make war against the Polish king. As the news spread the Poles rushed to defend their land. In a great battle on the plains, many on both sides were killed.

Then the emperor sent a messenger to the king. "Instead of killing so many of our brave men, why not each army choose one man? In single combat let these two fight. He who wins shall win for his army and for his land. If a German wins, Poland is mine. If a Pole should win, Poland is still yours."

Now the Polish king gladly agreed. By swift messenger he sent to the mountains for the bandit Jan. Yes, now, O Janosik, your king commands.

Janosik leaned on his axe. With the swiftness of wind he arrived on the battlefield. Mounted on his king's white horse, he rode out to meet the German soldier mounted on a black war steed, man and horse covered with steel armor. At the German's side hung a long sword, a sharp lance, a battle-axe, a knife. No wonder he laughed at the young Pole clad only in his white shirt, a curved knife in his broad leather belt, a hat with an eagle feather on his head, in his hand a mountain axe.

"Ha, ha," the armored soldier shouted to his emperor. "The victory is easily won, sire. Poland is yours."

"Watch and see," said Janosik, bowing to his king, "if the white eagle of Poland bows its head before any man."

Now the two rode off to opposite points of the field. The horses wheeled and came thundering on, meeting in a clash of splintering lances. To the German soldier's amazement, the white shirt of Janosik was as a shield of stone. Neither his lance pierced it, nor yet his sword. But since the magic axe could cleave metal, his own halbert was now split in two. And soon the great steel-clad form came crashing to earth at the highlander's feet. The emperor wheeled his mount. With a dark face he withdrew his hosts. The king of Poland had won. The invaders rode out of the land.

Then the king called Janosik to him. "Ask me a boon. I will give you whatever you wish : lands, palaces, money, gems."

But Janosik shook his head. "I fought not for price, sire, but for you, for Poland. What need have I for houses or lands ? The caves of the mountains are better than these. There I will live a free life with my men. There, only there is my home."

So Janosik bowed to his king, leaned on his axe, and flew back to our own Tatra peaks.

Everyone sighed. Ah, that was a tale.

"Someday, I think I should like to be a bandit, too," said Jasiek.

His father shook his head. "Then, there was no law of the land protecting the weak, the poor, the peasant on the soil. So Janosik made a law of his own. He and his merry men took the law into their own hands. But today, today we have the Seym, the Assembly chosen to make our laws. Let us be free, son, but let us also obey the law of our land."

"Well then, lad," said Grandfather, reaching for his bagpipe, "if you may not be a robber, you may still dance the bandit dance. Come, who says that a farmer, a peasant, a carver of wood called Jasiek may not dance the dance of bandits with the best of them!"

So Grandfather taught Jas the dance, and Hanka and Marta clapped their hands.

CHAPTER 11

Winter Fun

IF Marta shared in the indoor life during winter, she shared
also in the fun out of doors.   For sometimes there shone
a glittering sun.   Nothing hid its face.   It glistened down
on the snow so that the myriad crystals shone like jewels,
red, green, violet, amber, blue.

৵ঃ 95 ৪৹

Then the doors to all the steep-roofed mountain houses opened wide. Out came the children and young people. The boys skied down the steep slopes. With cheeks like red apples, Jasiek whooped as he skimmed. The older girls liked to ride in pretty carved sleighs, laughing as the wind whipped the snow into their faces. Marysia was one of these.

The small boys had sleds and went flying down the hills, often tumbling off in a whirl of powdery snow. Hanka laughed and laughed. She and Burek and Marta watched all the fun. She explained it all to her doll, the skiing, the sleighing, the sleds. Burek ran about sniffing his nose into the drifts and tossing the light snow into the air. He pranced and he danced. He lay down in it and rolled over and over. He was so happy in winter that almost he spoke in human speech.

Now he rushed back to Hanka, playfully reaching up to pull at Marta's foot. Hanka held her doll safely out of his reach, high above her head. So they played the game over and over. For Burek never tired of teasing his small mistress. He felt so good that he wanted Marta to play with.

Piotr, a neighbor boy, shouted, "Here, Hanka, come ride down the hill with us."

Hanka ran. Over her warm sheepskin coat, Grandmother had pinned a big shawl. Inside this she held Marta, kept warm from the cold. It was Marta's first ride. Oh! It took Hanka's breath to go so fast down the slope. The wind brought stinging tears.   The cold froze them fast to her red cheeks.   Her long shawl caught in the runners. The sled swirled to one side.   They went over in a bundle of children, shawls and dogs.   For Burek and his friends were racing alongside.

Everyone shouted with laughter.   What a spill, *hai-ji*! Hanka was eating snow.   She felt it trickling down her warm neck where the shawl had fallen loose over her head. She struggled to free her arms, bound fast in the shawl.

Then Burek pushed her over on her back in the deep snow. So she made an angel with wings.   Piotr made an angel, too.

"*Hai*, that was a good spill," Piotr exulted, struggling to his feet and pulling up Hanka.   "Come on, let's climb up for another slide."

"Let's!   And I'll help pull the sled," Hanka agreed.   It was the first time she had gone sledding like this with Piotr. It was such fun!

Again, get set, ready, go!   Whizz, they flew down the hill, this time, to a safe landing.   Up again, everybody off, and up we go.   Down and up, up and down.   And all this while the sun was traveling westward.   The snow had turned from pale yellow to lavender to light blue to shell pink.   The long shadows had changed from blue to pale purple.   The wind blew sharp and cold.

Marysia came back from her ride, the sleigh bells jingling, the little horse's flanks steaming.

"Why Hanka, are you still here?   Come home now,

there's a lamb. So you've been sliding all this time. What fun it is! But how draggled your shawl. See where the snow has packed down inside your boots, your feet must be soaked. Come along home. And Burek, you come too. There's a good dog."

But Burek put his tail between his legs as if he had been scolded and ran off by himself.

"He looks as if he had eaten a chicken again," Marysia said.

"But he was here with us all the while," Hanka told her sister. "He knocked me down in the snow, and I made an angel. And he tried to take Marta — "

She stopped, a cold terror at her heart. She opened her shawl and shook it. Marta! Where was she?

To Marysia's surprise, Hanka began running about like a small thing gone mad. She got down on her knees and clawed at the snow. She made a low sobbing, wailing sound from her heart. The boys, the children crowded about her. They searched too, up the hill and down, wherever the sled had foundered in deep snow, beside the smooth tracks. But no Marta.

It was such a sudden grief as Hanka could hardly bear. Marysia understood. She was sorry, but she knew, too, that Hanka was cold, tired, miserable. She must get home to the fire and dry her feet. But Hanka refused to go home without her doll. How could she leave Marta alone in the snowy world? So the little girl had to be dragged along, blind and deaf before such enormous grief. Marta gone, where? In the excitement of the fun, she had let Marta slip out of her arms. She had forgotten her, for almost the first time since she had come to live with Hanka.

Who could comfort her? Not Mother nor Babcia, nor Zosia nor Marysia, not Jasiek nor Father. Hanka sat bending over the empty cradle, and her woe was like a wave of the sea flowing over her, through her, around her. She could not eat, she could not talk.

But she could sleep. For when Mother finally tucked her into bed, she slept all the night through, and late into the next day.

As usual, on waking, she leaned over the side of her bed to see the cradle beneath, with Marta peacefully sleeping. Today, the cradle was empty. The terrible ache was still in her heart.

Hanka was a very quiet little girl now. She did not play. She stood at the double window, pressed against the frost ferns, watching the snow drift down. Fine dry flakes that filled in all the footprints in the road. Since her throat was sore, Mother would not let her go out. Marysia stroked her hair.

"No use wearing out your eyes, child. Jasiek has gone out to hunt. He took some of the boys with him. Let that comfort your heart, little Hanka."

When Jasiek came in stamping off the snow from his boots, she ran to meet him. But the boy shook his head.

"God pity you, Hanka. We poked all about where you were sliding. With our sharp axe-sticks we poked into the drifts, but no Marta. Burek helped us search."

But at sight of Hanka's tears, Burek put his tail between his legs and crouched at her feet.

"See, Hanka, even Burek is sorry. He, too, misses your doll." Truly he did seem to miss her, for he laid his head in the empty cradle, and looked at Hanka sorrowfully out of his brown eyes.

Mother and Father each said to Hanka what they would say to a neighbor who had lost a child. Yet this did not comfort Hanka as it perhaps should. So they reminded her that God likes happy people best. But this was no comfort, either.

That night two neighbor men came in to talk with Hanka's father. She sat beside her cradle paying no attention to them. Her thoughts were all with Marta. Was she sleeping under the snow, or awake? Had the wicked fairies or gnomes taken her away?

Suddenly she was aware of a feeling among the grown-ups. Her mother had put her apron over her head. That meant something was wrong. The men were all silent, pulling at their pipes. Jasiek had stopped his whittling, and Marysia her embroidery. Hanka stared from one face to another.

"When, how soon do you think war will come to our mountains?" Hanka heard her mother whisper, her hand over her mouth.

The men shrugged their shoulders. Who could say when? They fell to talking and Hanka opened wide her ears. The talk was all of guns, of bombs that dropped from the sky, yes, from big enemy planes that flew right over their peaks. Villages would burn. Families would scatter to the forests to live among the beasts. Lucky their hills had deep caves. Father might soon have to go to fight, to defend his land, perhaps even Jasiek, too. War was war.

Hanka thought that this war must be a terrible dragon still unslain in the world. She felt the terror of their hearts, an old terror of other days and of other wars before ever she had come to live on this Polish earth.

While they talked, Hanka slipped out unseen into the dark entryway. She caught up her mother's shawl. She unlatched the outer door. She ran across the yard to her own castle, over the snow hard and crusty, frosted in the moonlight and sparkling. She parted the branches heavy and white, and slipped inside. She sat down on the stump that had been their table when she and Marta had played at keeping house.

Now Marta was lost. And now the grown-ups were afraid because the black hour was creeping close upon them.

She heard the pounding of her heart, thump, thump, thump. She shivered under the warm shawl.

Soon she grew still, as still as the night. The thick branches shut her into a warm world of their own. Here she was safe, as unafraid as Pan Jezus in His mother's arms.

When war came, she would come here to hide. Here, nothing and no one could harm her. Here she would hide them all, her mother and Babcia, Marysia and little Zosia. She would guard the castle doorway and not let them take away her father or Jasiek. Inside the tree her whole family would be safe. They could build a little fire. Mother could cook the good soup. Here the bad enemy would never find them.

Now Hanka felt in her heart that Marta, too, must be safe. Surely, the Queen of Heaven herself would guard her. She could command all the fairies and gnomes to obey, yes, even the bad ones who hid Marta away. She who had stars in her eyes, who slept never at all, would come walking over the snow to the fairies' hiding place. In her arms she would lift Marta up and bring her safe home.

Now Hanka could hear the pine boughs whispering above her, and it was like the voice of Our Lady, whispering that it was so. For the first time, Hanka was comforted. She was no more afraid. Now she knew in her heart a peace which no loss, no grief could take away.

Parting the branches, Hanka stepped out into the crunchy snow, into the path of yellow light from the window.

As she ran in, the family looked up with startled faces. Was she a ghost then, coming in out of the night? All white with glistening snow?

Hanka laughed, a ringing, childish laugh that they had not heard for days.

"You needn't be afraid," she told them. "War will never

find us here, because I know a safe place where I can hide you. The Heavenly Queen herself has promised me. She will protect us all ; and she will surely bring Marta back home again."

Her father held out his arms and gathered the little daughter close. He said a Polish saying : "If you don't forget about God, God won't forget about you."

Then Mother served a cup of wodka to the grown-ups and a honey cake to each one.

So the deep sorrow lifted. The black hour of pain passed. With brave hearts they all said good night.

As for Hanka, she went to sleep cuddling her doll's small pillow. "She will come back to me," she kept whispering. "The dear Mother Marya will bring her. Or else she may send her home carried by good fairies."

CHAPTER 12

Star-Night

"CHRISTMAS is coming; Christmas is nearly here."
Every day Hanka told it to Zosia. For every child in
the mountains, the coming Star-Night, Christmas Eve, was
the most important night in all the year.

Zosia's big blue eyes opened wide. What was Christmas?

So Hanka told her. Inside there would be a Christmas tree, shining with lights. For supper on Star-Night, Mother would cook fish and honey cakes and *kluski*, made of broad noodles and poppy seeds. From outside would come the boys bearing a lighted star, singing carols and bringing in the puppet show.

Just then the happy light went out of Hanka's face. However would it be now to live through Christmas and Star-Night without Marta? She looked up at the carved blue Mother of God on the shelf. Not yet had she kept her promise made under the snowy spruce tree. Not yet had she brought home the lost doll.

Hanka threw herself down beside Burek, dozing before the hot stove. She whispered into his twitching ear, "If only Marta were here!"

Now as always, at mention of Marta, Burek put his tail between his legs and blinked his sad brown eyes. Truly he understood. Truly, Burek was their Polish nobleman, as Father always said. Hanka's eyes prickled with tears. She buried her face in the thick white and brown fur. "She promised to bring her home!"

But just then, Mother called Hanka to help. Indeed, she was kept so busy helping that before she knew it, the day before Christmas had arrived.

Now things began to happen very fast. Hanka must mind little Zosia because the grown-ups' hands were so busy with scrubbing and cooking.

Soon Jasiek came stomping in from the snowy world dragging a tree. A beautiful little red fir with perfect branches that just fitted atop the kitchen table.

He tried his best to keep the little sisters from peeking. He tied kerchiefs over their eyes while Mother and Babcia and he decorated the tree with bright red apples hanging from their stems ; with Marysia's colored candies and walnuts ; with paper chains, blue, red and yellow ; with Mother's funny little figures of Saint Nicholas cut out of gingerbread, so fragrant that they made Hanka's mouth water.

"But on this fasting day, we must not eat till the first star," she told Zosia. Mother said it, and Father, and Babcia and Marysia and Jasiek. They all said it, laughing and groaning, because of the fragrant pots already bubbling on the stove. "No, not till the first star."

Hanka pulled the small sister to the window to watch. Too soon. The sun was still riding high in the sky, still turning the white peaks to gold. The long shadows were still blue.

Now Jas brought in hay from the barnloft, fragrant and dry, to spread on the table. Over it Mother laid a clean cloth as white as a cloud.

"Because you know that Pan Jezus was born this glad night in a manger filled with hay," Mother said, laying the plates and the wooden spoons.

Hanka nodded. If only she could tell it to Marta, as she

had planned. If only the doll need not spend Star-Night alone, out there in the cold.

Then Grandfather arrived with every pocket bulging. Hanka and Zosia danced about him, feeling them. Burek sniffed at them, too. He kept leaping up, barking. He did like Grandfather so well, this dear Dziadek from over the mountain.

"Down, boy, down !" Grandfather begged. He smiled at the girls over the dog's big head. "Even Burek must fast till the first star shines clear."

"What, no star yet ?" cried Jas, rubbing his empty stomach.

So Hanka ran back to press her nose against the double window as she stared up into the deepening sky.

"All is ready," called Mother. "Here comes Father from feeding the beasts. Hanka, look sharp now, child."

"Oh, there, now I see it," Hanka shouted. "There it is, Mother ; the first star shines clear !"

Holy, wondrous sight, the first star on Star-Night, shining from out the blue bowl of heaven onto the blue and white world waiting below.

"Come to supper, then," Mother invited, from among the steaming fragrances on the stove. "Come one, come all. Jasiek, you may light the candles."

Now all the family gathered around the big kitchen table. They were eight, with an extra place set for the stranger who might knock at the door. Breathless, shining moment of the year, to watch as Jasiek lighted the tiny wax candles on the fragrant tree in their midst. How they shone on the red-cheeked apples, on the gingerbread saints. How they lighted up the goodies and the angel perched at the top !

Now Father broke a holy wafer which he shared with each one over a wish. Jasiek must take out a bit to the stable to give to the cows. The crumbs he would scatter to the birds, starlings and winter sparrows.

Now Mother began serving the good hot soup, the *barszcz*, full of red beets and yellow noodles and dark dried mushrooms. Soon the table groaned with the twelve dishes, one for each of the twelve Apostles, made of fish and mushrooms, of potatoes and cabbage. Not forgetting the *kluski*, broad noodles and poppy seeds.

What a merry supper it was. The fear of war was shut away. For this glad night all grown-up griefs were covered over, as the snow covered the earth. Only Hanka remembered her doll in the midst of the fun.

"You promised," she reminded the Lady in blue, holding her Babe.

After supper — and how much they all ate — Hanka watched again at the window for a star : not shining in the sky. Now she could see it, as yellow as a sun, far down the road. It was carried, she knew, by the neighbor boys, Jas and Piotr among them. For Jasiek had gulped the last bites of his supper. With a cake in one hand, and his flute in the

Now Hanka could see the star

other, he had rushed out to join the boys. This was their
own special night. Now Hanka could see the yellow star
moving up the road.

"They are coming!" she cried to the others. "The star
moves closer and closer."

Everyone came crowding before the window to see.
Burek barked and whined to be let out. Hanka begged to
go, too, but she was still too small, they all told her. So she
must stay close in the warm house, with all her family about
her, all but Jas, watching as the yellow star moved up the
road till it stood outside their own door. Jas was playing his
flute and Piotr his fiddle, while the others all shouted the
carol :

Amid the silence of the solemn night —

Little Zosia shouted in reply.

"Hush, child, listen," said Father, lifting her up in his
arms. "Hush. Hear the lovely carol. I sang it as a boy."

> *Amid the silence of the solemn night,*
> *Sound the angels singing,*
> *Lo, the King of Light !*
> *Rouse, O shepherds, haste with singing,*
> *Christ has come, salvation bringing,*
> *Born at Bethlehem.*

The young voices rang out over the frosty world, fresh,
hearty, gay. Hanka thought, "They sound like angels from

Paradise, but I know very well who they are, and I wish they would come right in."

Then, joy of joys, Father flung open the heavy door. Up the path of yellow lamplight Jas led the group, well muffled against the cold ; some in high fur hats. They all bowed.

"Jezus Christ is born." They shouted the good news.

From within, the family answered with a glad shout, "May His holy name be praised. Welcome and come in."

Hanka watched as the boys set up the puppet show, the wonderful Christmas *szopka*. Like a small wooden church it was, with a cleft floor through which the puppet sticks could be thrust from beneath. She had watched Jas carve some of them, small wooden figures, mounted on sticks. She knew very well which were the Holy Family, which the shepherds, and which the three kings. She pointed them out for Zosia, with the wicked King Herod and the black and red devil.

"But, oh, if only Marta could see them all, too."

As the smallest boy disappeared beneath the curtain, Hanka and Zosia sat down on the floor right in front. The others grouped about the little theatre. While Jasiek lighted the tiny stage candles, Father put out the lamp.

Then, even though the boys must speak the parts for the puppets, to Hanka they all became real people, acting out the story of Christmas just as it happened on Star-Night, long ago.

When small Mother Marya sang her lullaby, Hanka knew

it, too, by heart, all the verses. It was the very same cradle song she had sung so often to Marta.

> *Bring for the little man*
>   *good things and pleasant,*
> *Buy for the little man*
>   *every sweet berry.*
> *Into the garden go,*
>   *where all is pleasant ;*
> *Mary will comfort him,*
>   *keeping him merry.*

"If only Marta could hear it," Hanka whispered to herself. "If only Marta could hear them singing the carols !"

So Hanka could not help joining in. Soon Marysia sang too ; then Mother, then Father's deep voice, and Babcia's thin quaver, and Grandfather blew on his bagpipes. And as for Zosia, she clapped her fat hands, and made a song of her own, without words or a tune.

"But I think Pan Jezus and Mother Marya will understand it," Hanka said.

When the first act was over, as soon as ever the devil had cut off wicked King Herod's head, the speaking-line boys said they must go on to give the next act at a neighbor's house up the road. So Mother ran to bring out the honey cakes, one for every boy, and an apple as well. In the sudden silence of munching, there came a sound of scratching at the door.

"Burek wants to come in," said Hanka. "He wants to sing carols too."

"Make him brush off the snow, then," cautioned Mother.

Jasiek opened the door. But Burek bounded past him, straight up to Hanka. In his red mouth he carried an object, limp, dangling, wet, cold. He shook his head, and laid it at Hanka's feet. She gave a glad cry. She caught up the doll, damp, snowy, wet as it was and hugged it to her heart. It was Marta come home again !

The whole family crowded close to see. And while Hanka threw her arms around Burek's neck, all glistening with snow, Marysia quickly pulled off the doll's soggy dress. She smoothed down the tangled hair. She held Marta close to the stove to dry. She dressed her in a gay headkerchief of her own, blue with pink roses.

Hanka held out her arms. Though the doll's cheeks were very pale, though the blue eyes stuck fast shut in sleep, it was still her Marta, as cuddly and soft as ever. Marta had come home.

"Wherever did you find her, Burek ?" they all wanted to know.

"Bad dog," Jasiek scolded. "Did you bury her like a bone, and then go dig her up again because your conscience pricked you ?"

"Oh, no," said Hanka quickly. "It was the very Queen of Heaven herself who found her. She promised to bring her back to me. So she waited for Star-Night, for Christmas Eve, just to surprise me."

Hanka ran over to stand beneath the small blue figure on the shelf. "You must have told it to Burek instead of to the good fairies," she said in her clear voice. "I do thank you, dear Mother Marya, ever and ever so much. I 'll try never to lose her again as long as I live, for ever and ever, Amen."

Then she ran to show to Marta the tree with the hanging apples and nuts and colored chains. "And there, you shall even nibble one of Saint Nicholas' feet. And see, Marta, there, standing on the very top of the tree is the Christmas angel."

Now when everything was over on this blissful night, when the grown-ups were ready to ride down with the horse and the sleigh to the church below for the midnight celebration of the Shepherds' Mass, the *Pasterka*, they could not find Hanka. Long ago, Zosia had been tucked into her too-small-for-her cradle bed. Babcia's eyes were nodding shut, too. But Hanka, wherever was the child, now? And Marta, too? Surely not gone off up the road with the caroling boys?

No, at last Marysia found the child, under the table, her head on the low red bench. Marta was still held in her arms, fast asleep. The little girl's round cheeks were still flushed and smiling.

Father stooped and lifted them both in his arms. "Truly, for Hanka, this is the happiest Christmas of her life."

Mother nodded, her heart full, as she turned down the bed and covered them both for the night.

"She really believes that the Mother Mary sent back her doll."

"Well, then," said Father, "let us have her child's faith, too, that Poland will rise from her troubles, that we shall be no more slave men but free."

Babcia chimed in. "That Poland shall freely live at peace with her neighbors."

Marysia added, "That all men on earth shall be brothers: that after war shall come peace."

Glossary

Babcia	(*bob*-cha) grandmother
baca	(*bah*-tsa) head shepherd
barszcz	(barshch) beet soup
Batory	(bah-*tory*) King Stephen Batory
Boleslaw	(bol*es*-laf) a king's name
Bulanek	(boo-*wan*-ek) the horse's name
Burek	(*boo*r-ek) the dog's name
dobra nocka	(do-bra *nots*-ka) wedding-eve dance
Dziadek	(*jah*-dek) grandfather
hala	(hah-lah) mountain pasture
Hanka	(*hahn*-ka) girl's name
Jadwiga	(yad-*vee*ga) a queen's name
Janosik	(yahn-*o*-sheek) a bandit's name
Jan Perlowicz	(yahn per-*wo*-veech) a hero's name
Jas	(yash) nicknames of Jan (John)
Jasiek	(yash-yek)
Jezus	(yeh-zus) Jesus
Kazimir	(kah-zee-mir) a king's name
kluski	(*klus*-ki) noodle dish
kolacz	(ko-watsch) cake
Krakow	(kra-koof) old capital of Poland

Mamusia	(mah-*moo*-shya) little mother
Marya	(mah-rya) Mary
Marysia	(mahr-*ish*ya) nickname of Marya
mazur	(mah-zoor) a dance
mazurka	(mah-*zoor*-ka) a dance
Pan	(pahn) Mr.
Pani	(pahnee) Mrs.
Pasterka	(pas-*tair*-ka) Shepherds' Mass
Sejm	(seym, same) Parliament
szopka	(*shop*-ka) Christmas puppet-show
Tatra	(tah-tra) mountain range of the Carpathians
Zakopane	(zah-ko-*pah*-nee) mountain village
Zosia	(zo-shya) girl's name

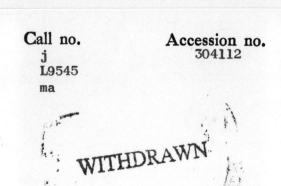